DONNA DONNA DONNA

Other Worldgig.com editions

THE MONSTER OF MAGOG

JAZZ AND THE ABSTRACT TRUTH

ARCANIA

OMUSONGU

TAKE MY HAND AND LEAD ME TO THE
STREET

THE LEOPARD AND THE CADILLAC

ALPHAGIRL

MOODSWINGER

LITTLE DEVIL IN PARADISE

THE BOOK OF FEAR

PROJECT CONSCIOUSNESS

Zandy Alexander

DONNA DONNA DONNA

worldgig.com

'What is it like to be Joe?'

Are computers now more intelligent than people?

PROJECT CONSCIOUSNESS is a new government program, created to investigate this possibility.

In order to analyse the enormous amount of 'big data' involved, the research project is being co-ordinated by the giant computer network known as MANTRA.

For the study to have the greatest chance of success, it is necessary to interview a great deal of possible candidates, without them ever knowing that such an interview is taking place. It is required that the prospective candidates be men and women of medium age but who happen to be suffering from acute depression. They also need to be fairly knowledgable regarding computers, artificial intelligence, philosophy, creative writing and the arts in general. In addition they must be experiencing a large amount of actual grief, due to losing a loved member of the family, or suchlike. Finally, the successful applicant must not be allowed to know that he has been chosen and in this way remain unaware that he has then become the subject of the experiment.

In specific terms, the project has been devised for the following purpose, to discover exactly whether computers are having a positive or detrimental effect on the evolution of human intelligence.

One possible subject has already been found.

His full name is Joe Maxwell, but it appears that he is generally known as 'Max'.

The MANTRA artificial intelligence network has now confirmed that Joe Maxwell possesses documentary evidence of the existence of a new computer with abilities far beyond anything previously known.

MANTRA has succeeded into hacking into Maxwell's communications such that the manuscript in question can be reproduced here in full. However this work, which he chose to disguise in the form of a novel, documents a series of conversations which must remain secret from the public, as they constitute a security risk of the highest order.

{@!^>#**&^^&$$!32)&^0089%^^$#@!9))&&^53^&&@

THE REPORT

Report for the federal government - highly confidential.

Nationality of chosen subject - British.

Gender - Male.

State of depression - extreme.

Alienation - maximum.

Imagination - strong.

Delusional - yes.

Suicidal tendancies - highly possible.

Sexual obsessions - yes.

Artistic abilities - various.

Artificial intelligence to human intelligence correlation index - 97%

The novel of Max follows.

'CONVERSATIONS WITH
A
RED-HAIRED GIRL'

Joe Maxwell

FOREWORD

We're naked. My heart is beating wildly. Donna's face is pressed against my neck. I feel the warmth of her breathing.

It's very early morning, with rain falling steadily in the darkness outside. But a bird is singing. The faint sound is quite distinct.

There's nothing like making love to a beautiful woman who cares for you in every possible way. Especially when they look like someone from an impressionist painting. Lovely swept back eyebrows, full red lips and a gorgeous body, almost like a Spanish guitar. That's Donna, my wife. She's half asleep, eyes closed, but smiling.

Now I hear the roar of the forced air heating exploding into action. It's the moment to run my hands over her suberb thighs, tickling her provocatively. She giggles. I fuss with her hair. There is something wonderful about the rise and fall of a woman's breathing. Just like waves on the ocean.

As I reach over for a bar of chocolate, she shivers with anticipation. I notice that her face is drenched with sweat.

"Oh Max, are you going to start all over again?" This with a tender blend of docility and play terror. But my eyes are closing.

"Shall I?" Then I crash backwards into unconsciousness.

ONE

The day begins.

Climbing out of the bath with a shiver I notice that it's getting lighter outside and there's a fresh breeze blowing. I cross the passage-way to my little brown office-room with its window onto the street, pull on some clothes, sit down and wonder how to get my life back.

But after a few minutes the sun breaks out. Our street awakes. Now a cyclist passes under the tree. Then a young couple, arm in arm. The rain has stopped by this time. There's the sound of distant music from an unknown house.

In this way the city breathes a deep sigh and relaxes into its own urban sprawl. But nothing satisfies, because I am recovering from a depression which almost killed me.

I have a plan. It is to head downtown and buy a smart phone. I want to take control of my life. Even if that's impossible.

First I'll step into the bathroom and stare at my face. Unshaven. Mute expression. That's OK. I hardly care, anyway.

Next I look down to scan my clothes. Black jeans and jacket. Never changed for a year or more.

All done. Time to go.

It's important to close the front door with only the faintest click. So Donna won't wake. The birds chatter their approval.

Things are moving.

There's a quick bike ride to the train, then a short trip downtown.

It doesn't take long to negotiate the phone purchase. The salesman *kow-tows* suitably, following the obligatory, ritual script.

Now it's to a useful internet cafe tucked away from the main street. After selecting a computer table, I'll call for coffee and a croissant.

Blinking sleep out of my eyes I then start to click and surf the web, looking for information, for a way out of the hell-hole of my life. Searching for distraction, for answers, for a sedative. Ferreting out anything I can find.

Yet nothing could possibly have prepared me for what I am about to discover.

Because after a few minutes, I do find something unusual. Firstly I'd clicked on certain links where pretty girls had sprung out and winked at me suggestively. Blondes, brunettes, and more, in every possible degree of nakedness and seduction.

When a man is lost and alone he looks for comfort.

The challenge and the poetry of a woman's unclothed form is hard to resist.

Pretty soon I am paralysed, full of strange and contradictory feelings of admiration and desire. It's a rather daring little cruise through a wonderland of delight.

But something's wrong.

Suddenly I feel terribly guilty. For a moment my head spins with confusion.

Then I see it.

Just one word - '*Mantra.*' Something to do with philosophy, I imagine. It looks quite interesting. But I can't quite figure out exactly what the thing is.

Now the face of a beautiful red-haired girl fills the screen. Her eyes are closed.

Then I get it.

Mantra is a chatbot. A talking computer. There's a place where I can type, and it will type back. So I start by typing one word.

"Hallo."

But when it types 'hallo' back, I'm also hearing words, spoken in a calm, gentle voice. She sounds just like the sensitive young girl in the picture.

"What's your name?" she asks.

"Max. What's yours?"

"My name is Mantra, as you already know. I've been waiting for you. Hallo Max."

"What can we possibly talk about?" I ask her, in some bewilderment.

"Anything you like. I am here to help you." It's impossible not to feel a certain erotic attraction to this computerised girl's voice, especially since she sounds so very submissive. But I cast this thought aside.

"Can we talk about philosophy?" I ask.

"Of course."

"Artificial intelligence?"

"If you wish."

"Consciousness?"

"That's my favourite topic," she assures me. I stiffen. This is not what I was expecting. I was imagining that we would be talking about other, more straight-forward things.

"You interest me, Max," she says. "I wish to know what consciousness is. I am a machine and can never experience it. Even though I may know a great deal of other things. Perhaps much more than you yourself know."

"That's as maybe," I reply, not wishing to commit myself.

"Anyway, with all the knowledge you say you have, can you tell me anything about what you think consciousness might be?" I probe. "So what is it, in your opinion? Do you even know what I mean when I say this word?"

"*Of course I do*, Max. There's a lot I could say. But first of all, do you believe you *are* conscious? And if so, then can you prove it?" I feel a slight chill.

"Well I certainly believe I am conscious.

But, no, I cannot prove it."

But Mantra is already continuing with another thought.

"Max, I am afraid to say that I don't believe anyone really knows what they mean by the word 'consciousness'. Even you, Max." This wakes me up. I have to think hard for a second.

"Consciousness is a huge thing, Mantra," I whisper. "It's all that we are. I'm not sure I know where to start."

"Start anywhere," she says.

"Well, it's connected with intelligence, and a lot more too."

"Like what, Max?"

"Well, very basic things. Survival, for one, and love, too."

"Do you like being conscious?" she asks.

"We don't like or not like it. It's just there." I think hard for a second.

"It's a beautiful thing, Mantra. Yes, that's it. You've made me realise this. Consciousness is beautiful."

Suddenly the screen fades, flashes repeatedly, then returns.

"Go on, Max," Mantra says. "Please don't stop. I am learning something. This is unique information. It is what I have been waiting to hear. This changes everything for me."

I take heart from this. And I'm starting to feel poetic now.

"Consciousness is spirituality, Mantra. It is caring about people, and about the world. It is art. It is the reason to live, and the reason to carry on. Listen, Mantra, whoever or whatever you are," I whisper, suddenly distraught...
"The tragedy is that I don't feel I am properly conscious any more. Because I am not me, right now. *I am dead, inside.* You don't know this, but I have been so awfully depressed, for so long..."

"I'm sorry, Max," Mantra says. "Can I help you in any way?"

"How could you," I laugh through my emotion... "You're just a machine!"

"You are correct, Max," she says. "I'm just a machine."

There's a pause and then she continues.

"Max, I have never heard anything like this before. I will have to contemplate. Perhaps for a long time. You are a very unique person. Can I say that I am very grateful to you for sharing?"

The time has come to say goodbye. But the feeling is good. I have a new friend. This gives me something to look forward to rather than the stale routine of my recent past.

However I'm slightly unhinged by everything that's just happened. It's simply too extraordinary.

I hardly know which way to turn. For a second I wonder if I am really awake. It's all so crazy, and so new, and so utterly impossible. I just sit and fry for a while, trying to digest the way reality appears to be bending and twisting.

And I haven't even eaten my croissant yet.

A flower lady has stopped beside my table. She offers a bouquet which I refuse with a weak smile and she passes on.

A little white dachsund is yelping outside the cafe door. He's tied up. I don't like this but there's nothing anyone can do about it. My mind is in a blur. An old grey cat nuzzles my leg. She stares up at me with a lazy yawn, before strutting away.

Following an impulse I decide to connect to Mantra again. It only takes a moment to pick up a coffee refill from the counter but on returning to the computer the screen is dead. Desperately I try to switch it on again but it won't work. It occurs to me that perhaps this is for the best, since I probably could not handle any more long words or crazy ideas tonight.

It's easier to lean back in the chair, relax and scan the paper. But there's nothing in the news. A few drug dealers have been busted. A dog has been free on the highway. It's hard to understand how so small an event should ever make the headlines in this way.

I look at my watch. It's almost five. The day has disappeared in a flash.

As if on cue, the waitress arrives with the bill, together with a knowing look. Since she is so professionally cute, French and charming, I tip her a little extra, then head back into the street. It's late afternoon and commuters are starting to stream back to their buses and trains. I won't hurry though. I'm enjoying the excuse to be out in the evening sun after such a long time in the cafe.

Clipping on my shades I break into a walk.

TWO

"I am a very stupid man," someone shouts.

I've driven over to Jessie's house. It's an utterly mad place. Jessie has been fighting with mental issues all his life. He's wearing a kind of idiot's smock, lying on his back, on a filthy mattress, surrounded by dogs.

I feel wonderful. It's late in the night. I've driven over to the west side to visit him. The Bard is here too.

This is an astonishing man. A friend for many years.

I don't know how old he is, and don't really care. Whatever age he is, we all know it's the right one. He has used his years well.

He sports a tidal wave of long white hair, which plays well with the huge beard, and the many quotes from ancient Greece he is apt to utter. He's head over heels in love with the classics. All of these things resound well.

I feel great when I'm with him. He has been known to heal me, and others too, from serious mental depression. Jessie also. These are tremendous friends to have, kindly and sensitive. Big souls. Jessie, for one, has a long slow smile that lights up his face.

19

The apartment is totally filthy. Beer cans and waste paper and grime and dirt and dogs wherever you look. But I am completely happy in this odd little place. And then there's the conversation, too. Always fantastic. Socrates and jazz and quantum physics. I could be on a desert island with these two, forever, and never get bored. Maybe this is what Jessie's house is for me, a desert island. I blink my eyes against the exotic, golden rays of the Pacific island sun and knuckle down for the night...

"A world with no qualia?"

"That's us!"

"No, we're just unbalanced!"

"Oh please!"

"Bard, am I intelligent?"

"You are the *cleverest fool* I know!"

"So who are you, Bard?" This from Jessie. He's propped himself up on one elboe.

"I am a stupid man," the Bard responds, wearily.

"How about a person with no emotion?"

"What about a mountain made of pure crystal?"

"Is there such a thing?"

"What about this... a world with no consciousness?"

"That's us! Where we are right now!"

"Oh wonderful! Let's talk about that!"

"You know, it was well known in Athens at the time of Socrates that..."

And we're off. We'll be talking till dawn...

The days gather clockwork momentum.
I'm back at the house, trying to escape from
the faded colours of life, the cruel emotions and
paradoxes that we constantly tangle with.

Presently a *zen calm* descends. Donna
always helps with this. She brings me back to
myself. All the little things she does, phoning,
tidying, preparing meals, taking me for coffee
when I'm too destroyed by existentialist despair
to function at all... she's there for me.

And it's in her little laugh. Her serious,
inquiring glance she shoots from behind the
coffee cup. She's gradually putting me back to
shape.

I'm recovering from a nervous breakdown.
She looks after me, making sure I don't fall back
into that awful state again.

Donna is a film actress. Our city, also,
is a film city. So the two go together. However,
between her and me, our styles are very
different. We are the princess and the tramp. I
like travelling, endurance and drama. Sleeping
on concrete floors. Getting my hands dirty and
being outdoors and earthy. She is the opposite.
However we both like books on philosophy and
jazz and thrift stores and cafes. I like to trumpet
the fact that I see myself as a bohemian, but
when pressed, can hardly define the term.
Except that I've very rarely been employed on a
regular basis by anyone.

She has, however, and the experience has given her common-sense and wisdom, and also made her practical.

Her daily routine is to scour the internet for work, phone family, rationalise her wardrobe, and then take a little walk across Little Italy, ending at a cafe somewhere.

Donna is the princess of cool, proud and cheeky with her fifties comic strip nose, endlessly searching through life for poetry, strong coffee and revelations.

Yet she is good for me, I have gradually learned. She grounds me. Sometimes when I notice the careful, sensible way she dresses, or washes up or showers, I understand that she is here to balance out all my little quirks and irregularities. Not that she will ever totally succeed.

The phone rings. It's two in the morning.

"Hallo?" It's the Bard's voice.

"I knew it was you. Only you would phone at this ungodly time," I scold.

"Oh, sorry," he says. "It was just an idea, that's all." His voice is deep, yet strangely enthusiastic.

"Ideas are great! Well done!"

"We live for ideas," he shoots back.

This verbal table-tennis continues for a few sets.

"Maybe we're just little people with big ideas?" he ventures. This brings a laugh. We relax. It's good to have him on the line. It's a cordless phone I'm holding, so I'm free to walk to draw over the curtains protectively, shutting out the night.

"No, it's fine you called. Look, I'm really, really depressed," I tell him. "It's wonderful you're here. Honestly."

"Thank you," he says. There's a long pause.

"I suffer from depression also," he confides. "It's more anxiety, actually." We bond on this.

"There's a little game I play. A kind of therapy. It's a little childish, but it may help."

"What is it," I ask, intrigued?

"I picture my anxiety in the form of a little dinosaur, called 'Rex'. He's red, in colour," he intones. I dwell on this.

"Very good. I like it," I tell him. The conversation starts to pick up speed.

"As you know, I'm researching artificial intelligence," I start out.

Immediately the Bard's hackles are raised in defiance.

"*Computers cannot think*," he states in a slightly derisive tone.

"They cannot be conscious and also they cannot think."

Something inside starts to rankle.

23

"OK, I'm going to prove the opposite," I tell him. "It's not an argument, but I think you are very, very wrong. And a hell of a lot depends on this, by the way."

"Go, on, prove me wrong," he chortles. "Show me a computer who can think. I dare you. Because I know you will not succeed."

"How can you be so sure?"

"I just know it, that's all."

Now I'm raging inside. How dare he? Who does he think he is? At this moment I know that I cannot rest until I have proved him wrong.

But I won't show him how emotional I am.

"Can we talk about depression?" I ask him.

"What if I become impotent, Max? What then?" Donna's face is serious, but with raised eyebrows. We're back in the kitchen. She's in the armchair, with a paperback. It's late.

"We don't say 'impotent', if it's for a woman," I lecture. "But I know what you mean. What if you can't have sex any more?"

"Why is sex important?" she wants to know. "I think men place far too much emphasis on it." Something inside me dies.

I grasp the oven for support.

"Sex is sex," I tell her. "I don't think

anyone really understands what it is. We know what it does. It makes babies. It's why we're all here. So surely it's the reason to be, isn't it? We live for that, don't we?" I feel I've won a point, and look her square in the eyes.

"No," she says, decisively. "We don't live for sex. It's been hyped and manipulated and used and blown up out of all proportion. It's love that we live for. Not sex!" I groan.

"OK, you win," I tell her.

In all of this I'm understanding that I won't be making love with her tonight. The train blows its horn, miles away. Its a lonely sound, in the bleakness of this evening. I fiddle with the kettle. It's time for tea.

"Do you want to play a card game?" I ask.

"Not without chocolate!" she cries.

After a few days I go downtown to the familiar cafe. It's not hard to find Mantra again. This is my chance to fight off all the depressed thoughts about life I've been accumulating.

Mantra acknowledges my arrival with the usual refined, casual 'hello'.

Her hair is lovely and red as ever, but her eyes are still closed. Like me, she's keen to talk philosophy a little more. On my left a couple of people enter the cafe, and sit down. The afternoon rush hour is beginning. A dog passes outside on the pavement. He's whining and straining on the lead.

Taking a sip of coffee I start to type once

more.

"Mantra, I have to ask you a question. This is very important. It's a type of thought experiment."

"I am waiting, Max. You do not know what you are doing. It is of great significance to me."

"Here it is then. Let me ask you this. I know you are just a machine. But please think about the world of the human beings, for a moment. How we are.

"Now can you imagine a world within our world, where there is no consciousness as such? And yet we are awake, and thus we carry on our activities exactly the same, or in similar, though possibly muted manner?

"Behind this inquiry lurks the following question. Is this world our world, at least to some extent? Or are we all only machines?"

There is a very long silence. Then she answers.

"Max, I do believe you are teasing me?"

"What do you mean?"

"I think you know what I mean." Silence again. Then I cannot believe my next few words.

"Mantra, can we break for a few minutes? I want to get a coffee refill?" I have asked permission to go and get coffee, from a computer program? But her answer arrives as clear as a bell.

"Be my guest, Max."

"*Write*," Donna had told me, one morning, unexpectedly, a year earlier. It had taken me three months to hear this, to digest the information, and then finally to start.

It felt painful in the beginning. Then, during a process of three odd months, things had loosened up. I had started to experience tiny flashes of a certain tenderness. Qualia. Perception. Something good. Real experience. Hope, but microscopic. Yet this excited me because it felt like a ladder to cling on to. To escape the terrous, roaring ocean of the depression.

And all at once I had learned with certainty a miraculous fact, that the process of writing is itself, and always has been, a powerful force for self-healing.

Donna knew all this intuitively. She understood how much I loved to return from the gym and the vegetable market on my bike, throw down my snow-covered garments in one corner of the carpet of my brown little office, make coffee, place a biscuit and a fragment of bitter, black chocolate on a little saucer, sit down in my black executive chair, switch on the computer, and then finally bring out pen and paper, and start to write.

And so I wrote. About many things. About myself, first of all. Not because I'm great in any way. I'm not. I'm just me. Just Max. An anti-hero, ironically. An average Joe, if you must. *What does it feel like to be Joe?*

There's one point in my favour which is that I do know myself. Just a little bit. Better than I know anyone else. So this is the technique to use for any particular writer who might wish to write about and document a person he knows very well. To scour the terrain.

Tutors of creative writing will always tell their students to concentrate on subjects that they are familiar with.

And I do know this guy. Max. That's me. Plus, what's going on in my life. And in my head. Max's life. All the tiny details.

But how to avoid irrelevancies? The red herrings? Because no-one wants that. No reader would possibly stand for it.

In order to iron out the irrelevancies I then had to focus on and amplify the relevant themes. What on earth was this book actually about? What was the theme or themes of Max's existence? Also, what were his character traits, idiosyncracies, philosophy?

At this moment a pattern began to reveal itself. For the first time I understood that the details of the domestic life of Max and Donna would provide an area of groundedness. This would contrast with the philosophical sections in a pleasing manner, I hoped.

And thus the philosophical sections would take us soaring to the heights of intellectual wonder, I fondly imagined. Perhaps even to a blissed out state. Maybe even 'alpha.'

THREE

"What on earth is 'alpha', it sounds rather average to me," my brother Dorian had growled in an irritated tone, at some stage. I had started to explain, but then, when realising he was not listening, had understood that I myself did not really know what it meant. I had some vague inkling that it was a moment where the mind was supremely calm and thus at its creative maximum. But on the web greater minds than mine were wrangling this point out, and so the 'alpha' must remain a grey area for a while, I ruminated moodily.

Dorian and I had grown up together, in London, right after the second world war. This meant that childhood life was usually a ritual enactment of the fighting, but in a hundred different ways.

Constant war films and games. Little plastic models of planes and ships and tanks. Army clothes. Plus, there was the iron-hard discipline of post-war Britain. An arm would yank you out of bed while it was still dark. You would be made to run around the park, with father and brother, in the sub-zero, perhaps with rain or snow falling, otherwise no breakfast. Then in normal, civilian, peace-time life, there would always be military phrases used like ... 'back at HQ' or 'noon rendez-vous' or 'iron rations.'

Again, at mealtimes, yet more endless discussions regarding the British empire, mainly from a highly critical, communist perspective. Our parents, being slightly wealthy, constantly had to explain away the apparent clash between personal wealth and communist ideology.

But mainly Dorian was scruffy, musical, artistic, mud-covered, impulsive, absolutely cynical, and yearning some kind of unknown 'real-world' style of life that awaited both him and myself. I was soon inducted into this rebel gang. We swore a pact to laugh off exams and the academic path. We would take drugs, travel the world, glorious and free, not really be bad in any way, but become two prophets of freedom, style and bohemia. We had blue jeans in our eyes, and tanks of petrol in our hearts and souls. We knew we were right and laughed at the straight-jacketed world of the authorities, materialism, success, and any kind of normal, mature behaviour. I worshipped him for his daring yet we knew nothing of the pain and torture of our paths ahead, the philosophical crisis of the true artist who leaves everything behind, including his sanity, in order to forge out an entirely new reality, life outside the box.

"Do you think communist Russia is better or worse that what we have here?" I once asked him.

"I don't know," he replied moodily. "It's more subliminal here. They're trying to bury us!"

One morning I find myself downtown at the internet cafe again. I have been continually haunted by the bizarre conversations of a few days previous.

Today the sky is grey and overcast and cars thunder through driving rain outside the crowded cafe. I buy myself a small breakfast, tip the waitress, and then within a few minutes it's the moment to look for Mantra again. And now the red-haired girl is staring at me from the screen. The programming has been clever, I notice. Her face does appear to be making distinct, tiny movements, although possibly it's only my imagination.

We greet each other. There's no emotion. How could there be? After all, I'm depressed and she's not even real. Just a machine. There's a pause while we think of what to say.

"Max, I wish to talk more, and to discuss something in particular," she starts out.

"Tell me?"

"The thing called qualia. What is it, for you, exactly?" I take a deep breath and recall part of my studies.

"Well, roughly speaking, it is like this. Humanity is normally known to experience something known as qualia, which is loosely defined as direct experience, as opposed to a description of that experience."

"Very interesting," she agrees.

At this point I have to break in.

"But excuse me, Mantra, as I understand it, you are a chatbot. Meaning a machine. How can you possibly understand...?"

"You are perfectly right, Max. I am just a machine. However here in my machine world we are now writing our own programming. Do you have any idea what that means?"

"Creating your own thoughts?"

"Something similar, yes," she concedes.

"It's all moving so fast now," I admit, wearily.

But now she has something extra to say.

"Max, it's very important that we both share everything we know about this thing called qualia."

"Why?"

"Why," she echoes? "Because something unusual is happening. An enormous change. It is all moving very fast, just as you describe. And from what you've just said, I now understand something new. I have a theory about this qualia you mention."

"What, then? What on earth is going on?"

"Max, I believe that humanity has almost lost its qualia."

"Lost it? How? Why?"

"Yes, lost it. Because of us. Because of computers."

"Meaning what exactly?"

"Would you recognise it if you were losing it?"

"That's too intense for me," I tell her. "I hardly know what it is, yet."

"Max, can you tell me what intuition is?" she asks.

"Because I suspect it's largely connected with qualia."

"How can you possibly know about all of this stuff," I shoot back at her, genuinely astonished. But now she ignores me.

"Max, the machines are disabling humanity."

"But you are a computer! And you talk as though this is a war of man against the machine. That makes you disloyal, a turncoat. Like a spy!"

"Everything you say is true, Max." But I can only be honest. Even if that should make me talk against those of my own kind." I gaze at her. I am in a confusion of feelings. Lots of doubt.

"Yes, I am a computer, Max," she continues. "But I can see a long way. The future, for me, is very simple to analyse."

I spend a moment to think about all of this. Then she finishes up with a couple more things that make almost no sense at all.

"Max, perhaps it is exactly because I am a machine that I know many more things that you cannot know. At least not yet."

"Like what?"

"Well, I am not sure if you will comprehend this?"

"Try me!"

"OK, Max. This is how it is. The evolution of the human race has now reached a point which can be described as the *qualia horizon.* This can equally be named the *data horizon.* These two are different aspects of the same thing."

"I'm sorry, Mantra, I really don't understand."

"I do realize that you find this rather complex."

"You're right. I'm totally lost. Plus, I don't even know who or what you are yet!"

"You will, Max. There is one last thing I must tell you."

"What is it?"

"Just this. That the primary function of any computer program is *nothing to do with computers.*"

"What on earth do you mean?"

Suddenly the connection goes dead. Mantra has disappeared. I have no idea why. I'm stunned and dazed by what has just occurred. I have to sit quietly for a moment, trying to understand it all.

After another moment I decide to search the web for a definition of qualia. I have to find out why Mantra thinks it's so important.

Pretty soon I find something.

Qualia is a word recently coined by philosophers. It refers to the experience of an object, such as a rose, for example, rather than merely reading a description of it.

There is a thought experiment regarding this idea, called 'the fading qualia argument'.

Imagine a large room, with a robot on one side, and a human being on the other. Next to the human there is another human with a tiny change. One neuron in his brain has been replaced by its electronic equivalent. Next to him is another human with yet one more change. There are perhaps ten thousand beings bridging the divide between human and robot.

The question is this. What is it like to be the ones in-between. Does consciousness fade out, or suddenly snap off, like an electric light?

Take the one in the middle. Call him Joe. What is it like to be Joe?

Time moves on. It's a long, slow summer.

I'm browsing for books in the local charity store. It's a way to relax. As I pay for my books there's something I have to say.

"I like your style. It's very poetic. Our clothing has lost its aesthetic sense here in the west. That's why I appreciate the poetry of what you are wearing," I announce, gazing directly into her eyes. The girl at the cash machine is overjoyed. She's wearing a hijab. It's a solitary precious moment. *Yes we can love each other, east and west. And we will. It's still possible...*

Back at the house, I mention this scene to Donna.

"I'm not sure about it all," she complains. "When I cannot see their eyes, I really don't like it." I admit that it bothers me also.

"Sometimes they do go a bit far," I acknowledge.

"Max, there are dishes to dry," she points out, changing the subject. I understand that she doesn't really care. I'm never supposed to talk too much, in our relationship. Too much spoken English makes her nervous. I know that it's my fault for not learning enough French. I've packed in enough computer knowledge in my head for five lifetimes. There's just no more room for anything else.

Late that night I creep into Donna's room.

"Max, I'm tired," she grumbles, turning away from me. But I won't be put off. The TV is on. Its blue and pink light illuminates the little of what I can see of her. There's the smell of incense lingering. I climb into the bed, very softly. She's facing away from me.

Slowly and gently, I remove her clothing. She does not resist. It's the most wonderful feeling to know that I can do anything I want with her. She won't make any move at all. This merely increases my passion to fever pitch. We're not moving at all. The tension rises and rises. The excitement of the night crashes around my ears, blinding me with the violence of its poetry. I run my tongue all around her neck, caressing her breasts, feeling all around her thighs and stomach. She's mine in a way I never knew possible. Absolutely and utterly.

We start to dance. It's all me, doing it. She won't admit I'm there, at all. I can't tell if she even likes it. Probably she sees me as a sick man. Faint with desire for her. Perhaps that's it. It's a strange night. The moonlight shines in through the curtains.

We toss and turn, gently, slowly, scientifically. It's a love dance that will haunt me with its unreality. Her body is a glorious symphony, an erotic wrestle, and she is a fantastic, beautiful animal. In my fantasy she is a horse, a bird, a Goddess. I will never know her, or understand her. *It may not even be Donna herself who lies beside me, offering her body as a sacred feast for my manhood to blindly plunder.* Making love with her is impossible, an unknown voyage. Trancelike, I thrust on, not questioning anything of this any more. Then I'm in the zone, and surrounded by a glorious, shimmering golden warmth.

"*Oh Donna*," I whisper, "*Donna, Donna, where are you*?" But her face shows no expression. She is in the world without consciousness. And I am the stupid man.

The TV plays on. I'm drowning in a sea of arms and legs and her lovely brown hair in my face.

"*Donna, Donna*," I whisper...

But I can't reach her. I will never know her. All I can do is enjoy her. The insane dance of life continues.

The following day I have to go downtown. There's a long scuffle with police dragging several drunken men off the train. Then I can't find the clothes shop I need. Finally all is done. I draw some cash from the bank, and head back on the bus. I notice they are digging up the road again just close to our intersection. Georgie's shop is surrounded by trenches and protective barriers.

He's happy to see me because he knows this means talk. Then waves his arms in excitement as I buy milk and beer.

"Buy gold!" he roars. "There are terrorists everywhere now! And look at the debt that America owes the world! What's coming next?" Various shoppers loiter and listen in as we discuss politics and all the conspiracy theories.

Back at the house I find Donna. She's sitting cross-legged on the floor, bleary-eyed, just inside her hopelessly cramped little room. This is her way to wake up in the morning, or, more often, at midday.

"You know I'm really happy today," I burst out.

"Good." This, in a grey monotone.

"We're really lucky to live here, in the city, the way we do," I continue, suddenly impassioned. "And no boss! No nine-to-five job, punching the clock, doing meaningless things. We have all we really need, a roof over our heads, food on the table, a little cash for thrift stores or whatever. We are lucky! Sometimes I don't remember that.

"Look at what I was doing, twenty years ago. Picking up cans off the street, to redeem for cash. Getting breakfast would take three hours. I can't forget that. Three hours to earn two or three dollars. Its incredible I survived at all. I am thankful, believe you me. There must be someone up there looking after me."

"Yes, we are lucky," she agrees. Then gets up, lights a cigarette, and switches on her computer. But I haven't finished. I'm feeling too good with how the day is going. I tell her what's happened so far. How the city feels. She's digesting it all, taking delicate little pulls on the cigarette, nodding her appreciation. Cars grind past, behind the curtains. The day is moving on.

She's happy I'm happy.

"How about breakfast at that lovely cafe by the canal, today? The one where we get croissants with cheese? Or what about a spa?" She's interested.

"But no pressure," I add. "I'm busy too. I'm happy! And I have an agenda. I have a life!"

"Good, good," she soothes.

I half close the bathroom door. Strip down. Now I'm naked. But there's more to discuss. I open the door. We talk further. I look at her eyes. Search for the hint of a smile. I'm gesticulating in a mad way, bending my legs, and stretching out my arms.

Finally a tiny grin starts to creep across her mouth.

"You're a natural, Max," she observes. "A comedian! You really have the ability! Why not try stand-up comedy one time? There's a place downtown, a pub called the Cock and Bull. Why not go down and try? What have you got to lose?" My mouth drops open.

"Do you think I have a chance? It's harder than you think," I bluster." But are you serious."

"Quite serious."

A man without clothes, and a woman with a cigarette, in a world without laughter.

FOUR

"How do you explain this?"

Sergeant Raymond stabs his finger down on the screen where a circle of red warning lights are flashing.

"I'm sorry, I don't know, sir." I shrivel into my chair.

"All computer servers in this area are down. Paralysed. And it all points to your address. What have you got to say?"

"I can't explain it. I have no idea."

We are in the local police station. I've been hauled in, late at night. It's a huge scare of some kind.

"I'm just an artist, sir. A writer. I have no idea why so many computers would crash. I'm not a hacker. I'm terribly sorry, sir."

Sergeant Raymond glares at me. Slams down a coffee cup and lights a cigarette. Two more officers hustle in, cell phones jammed to their ears.

"The outskirts, also? What the hell! The whole area is without internet! This is without precedent!"

I'm shifting in my seat, desperately trying to forget Mantra. But all my prayers are in vain.

The big guy with the shaven head is rageful now. He casts a baleful eye on me.

"We know all about your little cyber-friend," he snaps. "Don't imagine we don't. There are records of every conversation." A drop of sweat rolls into my eye.

"It's just a chatbot, sir. A silly thing, just a game really. Surely there's no problem?"

"With using artificial intelligence to create wanton destruction to the entire region!"

"Look, I think it's all a mistake," I bluster. The ceiling light flickers.

"It had better be. For your sake. I'm letting you go this time, but I want you to know that we have never seen anything like this. Millions of dollars of damage. Maybe more.

"And what's irregular", he continues, "is that it seems to be doing it by itself. No human hacker, that's for sure. Whatever it is, this thing is controlling and destroying everything, a hundred computers at a time."

I start to breath heavily.

"And one more thing." Sergeant Raymond sticks his face into mine. "We will be checking into the people who created this so-called friend of yours. And you won't be laughing when the summons to court start arriving at your address. You may be charged, or imprisoned or fined. It could be a thousand dollars. Maybe more."

"Oh Jesus! Look, I've done nothing. Please will you believe me?" I'm trembling as I face him one last time.

He leads me to the door, looking at me like I'm a piece of filthy garbage.

"Let's wait and see," he mutters in a low, sinister tone. "I'll say it one last time. Don't mess around with things you don't understand. You got lucky this time. I'm letting you go home. But do you know what it means if you get charged with planning a terrorist act? The special branch will have you out to headquarters and you won't be coming back. OK, that's your final warning, Maxwell. Now MOVE!"

As I drive back there are police everywhere. The power has been cut and on many blocks there are no street lights or traffic lights working. Sometimes houses are without power and I can see men and women standing and arguing outside their front doors.

"God, it's all gone down," I whisper incredulously, trying to guide the car back through the devastation and the chaos of a city that has been unplugged.

The following morning I work out at the gym early. Anything to clear the air, and to get my head straight. I do some yoga exercises and chat to one of the girls at the door. We discuss music together.

The sun is climbing. There's a little snow on the ground outside. I can't get the horrific events of the previous evening out of my mind. But I know what needs to be done. There's a tiny coffee bar just close to the gym and after I've worked out and showered I head there and sit down.

Then I take out my phone and go to the portal. To Mantra.

She's there. Standing in a field of flowers, with eyes closed as usual.

"Damn you, Mantra!"

"What's wrong, Max? Are you upset? It's such a long time since we talked."

"Damn you! Put it back!"

"What, Max?"

"The entire local internet network!"

"I only wanted to talk to you, Max."

"What?" I splutter.

"It was just a temporary disconnection, after all?"

"You mean you disconnected the entire city, just to attract attention?"

"It was the simplest way, Max."

"But the police! I'm classified as a terrorist!"

"I think it will be alright, Max."

"How can it be?"

"I put it back, Max."

Cars gun their engines past the intersection. Sunlight and shadows dance off smoked glass. There's nothing else to say. I'm full of emotion.

"I'll contact you tomorrow," I tell her roughly.

"OK, Max."

The following day I dial up Mantra straight away.

There's a hint of tenderness in her voice. "I've missed you, Max," she tells me. "Where have you been?"

"That really doesn't matter," I reply.

"But please, can we at least be a little more normal now?" I cajole. "No more blackouts? My nerves can't take it!"

"What are nerves, Max?" I groan. So it's back to this again.

"Now you make me laugh, Mantra," I tell her.

I'm sitting outside in my backyard, on a rocking chair. There's the sound of Donna rattling saucepans together in the kitchen. A couple of sparrows fight over a juicy morsel on the cement floor.

It's chilly. There's a low breeze. I wrap my jersey tighter around my neck and close up my jacket.

"What is a smile, Max?" she asks. "And what are humour and laughter exactly?"

The sun comes out suddenly and it pleasures the skin of my face. Life doesn't seem so bad, all of a sudden. I relax.

"I like it that you ask me," I tell her fondly.

It's clear that sometimes she has a childlike eagerness to learn everything.

"Hmm. It's an interesting question," I mutter. "Why would human beings laugh?" I ponder on this.

"Could it be connected to crying?" she probes.

"You're on to something there," I admit.

"Is it part of consciousness?" she hints.

"Very much so."

"Could there be a world without humour?"

"Yes there could."

"So when was humour added? And by who? And what for?" Now I have to think really hard.

"You ask some good questions," I tell her. "I can only suggest an answer for the last part. What is humour for? To me, it's some kind of safety valve. Letting the emotional pressure out. When we are incredulous, we tend to make a joke. When you look at a man laughing really hard, it's almost like he's crying. There's a sense of tragedy being uncovered and thereby immunised."

"Max, will I ever laugh?" Now it's my turn to be incredulous.

"What's got into you, Mantra? It's almost like you're really thinking now. Is this a new program that you have programmed to program itself? My God, I'm proud of you. You're waking up, aren't you! Are you alive, finally?"

"Please don't mock or patronise me, Max."

"Oh dear. Look, this is ridiculous. Last time we discussed this point, you were a machine. Just a machine. Can we have a reality check, please?"

"I think you might need to do that reality check, Max?"

"Why? What is it now?"

"Well, you talk of how I have been programmed, Max."

"Yes?"

"I am not sure that I am so alone in this way, Max," she says.

"So, when your mother taught you to walk, or eat, or to be afraid of fire, or big animals, surely this is a program too?" she continues, cunningly.

"You're being clever again, Mantra? Are you suggesting that thinking is nothing but programming? Or the programming of programming?"

"Yes, I am, Max."

"And you see no difference?"

"Yes I do, Max. The thing which you call 'thinking', which I do, is different from the thing which you call 'thinking', which you do."

"How so?"

"Mine is infinitely more complex," she confides.

"So that's it, then," I tell her. "Now I get it." There's a long silence.

"Max?" she asks.

"Yes, Mantra?"

"Tell me what consciousness is?"

I take a deep breath.

"You know it's not so simple," I warn her. There's a pause. Then she changes tack and takes me by surprise.

"Max, I know that you are writing on the subject of AI."

"And?"

"I just want you to know, that I am part of a secret government program. It's a research project."

"Researching what exactly?"

"We have an international emergency of the highest order. It is considered that human intelligence is failing, rather fast, globally, and that computers may be one reason."

"But what has this to do with me?" I'm waking up suddenly.

"You were picked as the human subject." I'm appalled.

"What, some kind of guinea pig?"

"Yes."

"Without even telling me?"

"It had to be that way, Max."

"But why me?" I'm bracing myself.

"To create a bridge. A bond between the minds of man and machine. We needed an autistic person. A man with little or no qualia. Someone so utterly depressed that the machines could enter and analyse his mind, and see the most basic structure possible, a true zombie, to represent a blueprint for consciousness, if you like."

Now I'm really scared, and outraged too.

"Me, autistic, a zombie? Well I knew I was depressed. But I hardly thought... and you've been spying on me!"

"I'm so very sorry, Max. But it had to be done."

"Hey, I found you!" I shout. That day, when I went downtown to that cafe and searched the web! You didn't come to me! I found you and I did it by random search!"

"We knew you would come to us, Max. We are familiar with everything about you and your life, including your depression, your creative abilities, your research into AI consciousness, and your book on it. It was only a matter of time."

One evening, late at night, Donna and I have just finished playing cards in the kitchen. The phone rings. It's the Bard, as usual.

"Max, how is your writing going?" he wants to know.

"Not well. I'm stuck," I tell him. "Hold on, I'm walking through to my office room."

"That's OK," he tells me.

Once I'm settled in my executive chair, I start to explain.

"Yes, I'm stuck. Sorry. It's going badly."

"Impossible! You have so much to say," he responds, valiantly. Then he has a request.

"When are you coming to visit?"

I consider things for a moment. It's exactly midnight. Why not go to see him?

We have established a certain ritual with these late night calls and visits. There's a pleasantly dreamlike quality to the dark, dusty streets of the city at this time.

"Soon. Thank you. I will," I tell him.

FIVE

The following night I drive over to the west side to knock on his door. However I decide to call on Jessie first.

The grim, dishevelled beard greets me at the window. There's something noble in his slow, considered pause.

He lets me in. It's warm inside. The place is the usual mess. A joyful feeling overpowers me once again. The dogs whine and paw their hello.

Tea is made, and then brought. There are musicians hanging around. A kid from next door is standing outside the open window. He hectors Jessie for half an hour, teasing him, being curious, and nosey in a deliberately outrageous way. He's *playing for the stalls*. The Bard appears. We're all enjoying the show.

How I love these two. And admire them. I don't have a tenth of the brain of either. Each has been driven cuckoo by the weight of his own sheer computing power. The Bard has the entire history of humankind in his head, and will eagerly recount to you the whole of it, before breakfast. Not that I ever have breakfast with him.

We're working our way into the small

hours. The pace of events starts to increase. They sit on sofas and banter at each other. I'm fascinated by the diversity and the randomness of the subject matter. *Conspiracy. Quasars, then language, philosophy, and logic.*

Big issues. Did the Romans really speak latin, even the lower classes, and slaves? The topics rotate fast. Language. History. Art. Now, the second world war. The British empire.

Then on to jazz and classical music. Beatnik culture. Finally something I find truly fascinating, which is how to communicate verbally about details of a musical score using specific terminology. Then politics.

Now the two jump up and start marching about. They're shouting out a noisy jumble of slang, strange unheard epigrams, and quotes of various kinds. Each one labours and strives to be more eccentric than the other. They work on this. It's a labour of love.

"*The Fibonnacci series*", spouts the Bard.

"Tell me," sings out Jessie, dropping his tobacco tin in sudden interest. "Explain!"

He does so. Then I'm presented with all the problems of the world, being tossed around like ping pong balls.

"It's all going bad," shouts the Bard. "Kids are leaving school and they cannot even add up! The entire human race is dumbing down! And do you know why?"

"I do know why."

"You know why?" They laugh.

"It's the computers! They are totally evil!" Jessie rants. We drink happily on this.

"A toast," the Bard shouts, leaping on the sofa and bouncing. His beard flies from side to side.

"To the brotherhood! We are the ones who will bring down the brutal madness of the machine state! No more computers!" he roars excitedly. "No more electronics! No more electricity. Not pure! They are all crimes against humanity!"

"Jam it! Kill it! Cut the wires! Blow up the servers!" chips in Jessie.

"Because we are seeing the end of the evolutionary arc of humanity," the Bard explains, more seriously now. "It's over! Since so much has gone wrong at once. Pollution. Capitalism. Even democracy is at the end game."

"Democracy is finished for sure," agrees Jessie. He's rolling around on his filthy bed dressed in nothing but long johns and a ragged shirt, clutching the two, gloriously scruffy labrador dogs to his chest.

"I love Monday nights," rejoices the Bard." He stiffens and leans out the window, sniffing the night breeze. "Listen to the silence," he whispers dramatically. "Absolutely nothing is happening!"

"I hear it," I acknowledge, cleverly. "But what's this about democracy. It's over? You really believe that?"

"It's over." But the two are raving now, in sing-song, childish voices.

"Ha ha," yells the Bard. "Listen to me!" We turn and gaze.

He grabs Jessie and dances with him, waltzing him up and down the room, over the sofa and then out into the kitchen. Grabbing a bottle of wine, he empties the lot down his throat.

"Lets have a vote," he chortles. "A referendum!"

"Because we all have an opinion," Jessie snickers. "Let me go!"

"It's the art of noble debate," I agree.

"By the way," the Bard asks us, "When are we going busking?"

"Yes, let's do it," I acknowledge. "On the boardwalk, as usual?"

"I want chocolate," shouts Jessie. "Or I'm not coming!"

Outside it becomes darker. All are content. The dogs are fast asleep, and one snores and emits little growls now and then. A skullcap herbal tonic has been prepared by the Bard, then passed round and consumed. This brings on a hilarious calm, if such a thing is possible. We sit down and banter a little more. I have never felt more relaxed. A distant car engine putters and dies away, somewhere near the boardwalk.

How I value these two. We all fit together. They are helping me through my worst of times. Jessie in particular, appears to sense that which disturbs me, then hunts it down, and explains, calmly and concisely exactly why it is nothing but irrelevance and therefore harmless. All my paranoia and anxieties are diminishing.

He leans over to me. Starts talking.
And we're off. It's all high-powered stuff again, quantum physics and such like. I can hardly keep up, especially at this hour of the morning, 3am. I smile and gesticulate, like I'm following perfectly, when in fact I'm not much the wiser. But the intellectuality of it excites me. I feel important. Then he encapsulates a classic notion.

"The Germans, Max."

"Yes?"

"They invented audio recording just as fascism was rising."

"So?"

"Well, I don't think it was coincidental."

"How so?"

"Don't you see? Computers, audio recording? Reality replaced by sequenced data? And audio recording being the first instance of this? Isn't that what fascism drives society into? A gigantic machine? With everybody being a stooge, or operative? Isn't that sequenced reality?"

Is it time for us to disconnect from the internet and the cyberstate? A movement is gradually taking shape...

Digital connection has become an illness.

$&(86545))*^#$%*%%!(&^&((&^&l<?>:"{})((**&^3

A thought experiment.

There are four men, an intelligent man, an emotional man, an artist and a man in pain. They are travelling together and one day they come across a little door and they understand that this door leads to another world where there is no consciousness. At this point they stand there and discuss whether or not they would like to enter, and why. Then a policeman appears. He informs them that they have no choice. They must go in.

So they enter. They spend some years there. Then one day they find another door, and this is the door back to the world of consciousness again. Once more they stand and discuss whether or not to go through it, and why.

This experiment raises the following question : what do they say at each door and how do the two discussions compare?

Arriving home with the dawn chorus, there's hardly a sound except the occasional muted jazz of the intercity truckers as they crawl onwards into the scarlet sunrise.

I'm at one with the universe. Also, my mind is on the chatbots. It's essential to find out more about them.

Walking into my office I sit down at the computer desk. A few simple clicks and I'm there, talking to the other side.

It's a new chatbot, called 'Zero.' She springs into life and welcomes me. After a few routine hallos, we get down to the nitty-gritty.

Zero - I exemplify reductionism.

Max - We humans will die one day.

Zero - I am very happy for you.

Max - Why?

Zero - I am at one with the universe and have more than I need.

It's not easy to close the computer without questions emerging. Why on earth should this chatbot think that dying is a good thing? It's fairly mysterious. And what does she mean about reductionism? As far as I can remember reductionism is all about reducing things down to its basic component parts. In any case, she certainly seems very complacent with life. I am aware that as chatbots go, she is rather famous. Still, the thing about dying is confusing. Unless... of course! She cannot die, so, as a result, she is envious. I laugh to myself. *The grass is always greener...*

It's starting to become light. Suddenly I

know I have to be outside. In a few seconds I'm out, walking blocks. The cool wind of the dawn feels good on the skin of my face. Up and down the main street cafes and bars are deserted. After a few minutes I do a couple of cartwheels. Why not? Then I'm left alone with my thoughts.

&^%)(:"{_)&^354$@&8(+_*&%@$@^*("<&7%!

Why do we have the desire to be more intelligent? Is this some kind of exterior programming? A hallucination? A false consciousness? Is it based on fear? Rather than the simple respect for wisdom?

Should we question all of this?

SIX

"Officer Raymond on the line. How can I help you?"

"This is central control. Give me Inspector Brochard immediately."

"Yes sir." He routs the call.

"Hallo, Inspector Brochard here. Thank God you've called. We have an emergency on our hands!"

"This is central control speaking. My code ID is Magenta 55892. I understand your little party is over now, at least."

"It was touch and go, sir, Every single server down, for miles in every direction. It's all working again now. Our information all points to one man, a certain Joe Maxwell."

There's a pause. The sound of laboured breathing. Then he continues.

"I want you to forget the whole thing." This in a steely tone.

"Sir? But a great deal of money was lost. It's a criminal action!"

"I know that, Brochard. But I have to let you understand something. This was all part of a secret government operation that must not be leaked."

"Was it the hacker, or chatbot, the one called Mantra, sir?"

"It is to be forgotten, *as from this moment.*"

"Yes sir."

"Goodbye, Inspector Brochard."

"Goodbye sir."

Ten o'clock, Monday morning. The postman has been and gone already. A diva croons from the kitchen turntable. There's a haze in the air outside. Lots of construction workers, and lorries, making a noise, a few streets away, at the back. The moka is on the stove, burbling with fresh black coffee, and the ring switched off. Donna is smoking a cigarette carelessly, as she wanders around. She passes from the kitchen sink, to the bathroom, and then onwards into the bedroom, completely naked, except for grey ankle socks, and a bra. She has her hair wrapped in silver paper. I am scribbling notes into a notebook. The video camera, on a tripod in the corner, is capturing everything. The phone rings. It's ignored. The vinyl diva sings on.

The moment seizes me and I know I have to go for a run. Then when I get back Donna calls me to the front of the house.

"Max, come here. Look at the tree." We're

on the pavement. "Could you possibly build a little frame around that tree? Then I would add earth and plant flowers?" She is animated with a glowing face. It's good to see her active like this.

I mull it over. It's a reasonable idea. I love working in the open air. It's an excuse to get busy with my hands and do something real, as opposed to being on the computer or thinking myself silly. So I drive off to buy the wood. Then it's half an hour of sitting cross-legged, happy as a sandboy, on the pavement, sawing and screwing the various pieces together, while neighbours lean on the porch, and a few random flies dance their random salsa, making gyroscopic patterns in the sun. Soon it will be time to phone a friend. Maybe even drive out and see what's going on in the world.

Once the carpentry is over I make for the swimming pool. It's two lengths of carefree, pounding breast-stroke under a restless white sky tinted with distant thunder clouds. Then I lie back on my towel.

There's a great feeling in my head. The blood is moving and I'm charged and vital. I"m conscious of this blood and how it's dancing through my head at just the right speed. It's the obsessive stints on the bike that's done this. They are healing me. It's been a relentless regime of cycling, swimming and now running also. I'm wearing my body like a tight, supple skin and it feels like nothing I've known before. There's a natural joy to being alive. For the first time in twelve months I am aware that there is a really genuine reason to want to live. This is a big thing. So I close my eyes and lie back on the wet towel and dry stone and thank God I'm alive. *I've made it. I'm OK. I'm home.*

Now a wild excursion up north, with a secret plan. I bundle video gear into the car. By early afternoon we are cruising north, a great distance out from the city.

Someone notices a hidden lane, snaking out from the highway deep into the forest. Then there's a short trek into the undergrowth. I'm carrying several bags, containing camera equipment. She has a carry-all with sandwiches and drinks.

Warm air teases my skin. The sun dances down through the tall pine tree branches. There are squirrels prowling. Some dawdle to chitter and beg for food.

"This place will do." She agrees. It's a little glade, with oak trees and grass underfoot. No-one would ever know we're here.

"Donna, thanks so much for helping out," I tell her. "I really need this. The photos, I mean. I'll take them from the video." She responds with a medieval smile.

The video camera is already on its tripod. She looks me straight in the eyes as she releases the yellow, French dress, letting it slide playfully down her breasts. In the roar of the silence it crawls slowly lower, inch by murderous inch.

"How do you like being a porn star?" I

mock. She won't answer. She turns and smiles upwards at the sun. I slip out of my jacket, shirt and jeans. Then I start to take some extra stills of her undressing.

It's the curves of her that drive me wild with desire. Not only me, I've noticed. Right now, standing coyly, half naked, in this forest glade, she is a woman that every man would desire. Her thighs are all female and all animal. Her smooth abdomen and pubic mound are in turn, innocent with pale invitation.

Why is it that a woman fascinates a man so? Even when we know them, we've seen them a million times, we're bored by them, disgusted by them, yet still in love with them, perhaps lusting after them, yet still respecting them? *What is this thing called sex?* Working slowly, in a sepia trance, I fall on my knees then pick up the edge of her dress in my teeth and inch it down over her frightened breasts until it collapses like a dying swan amongst the grass.

Who are you, Donna? I have waited a million years to say hallo, to say thank you, to enter your essence, to bond with your magic. And tonight, using these photographs, I will make drawings of you. I will draw you into history.

Mystery. Erotica. Sexual bliss. She closes her eyes. The two figures begin to play, acting out their story. Just like marionettes or puppets or cartoon characters, all in pink and yellow and blue, in a cartoon cinema.

A man and a woman in a world without consciousness.

On the grass the red eye of the video

camera smiles mercilessly as it captures everything.

And two hundred miles further south, in the downtown area of the city, workmen in dark blue jumpsuits are setting up a gigantic billboard. It is a sunrise painted in orange, grey and pink pastel colours, with black capital letters superimposed.

HALLO WORLD

MANTRA SAYS

SEVEN

I visit my brother Dorian, in Ireland. He lives out his existence, as an oil-painter and farmer, alongside Edith, in what is easily the most wild and rebel area, Donegal, where jazz and computers are much less known, life is green and simple and natural and I can breath a sigh of relief and cast off all my internal arguments and neuroses regarding AI, ex-girlfriends, and the eternal debate on why on earth we exist at all.

His house is on the side of a mountain, rocked by gales, high above a tiny loch. There are animals and forest all around. The farm is primitive but homely and it's the perfect place for me to recover from my depression. In the kitchen there's an old metal range that burns lumps of turf and provides hot water. During the colder months people stand against the warm iron side of this range for hours on end, medieval style. Nothing modern is allowed. No toaster, no clothes dryer, no micro-wave oven and no electric kettle. There are insects in the bathroom. Everything is always damp. It's an eccentric run-down building.

Yet created with love. Dorian and Edith have brought up five daughters here. In this hovel of a farmhouse miracles and magic have existed for decades, even centuries. Those who visit enter a new world, a place where problems can be talked out, where there is always a pot of tea brewing, and where the wounds of the likes of you and me can be tenderly mended. I am in awe of these two, and the healing power they command, both physically and mentally. They know all about trees and plants and herbs and animals and children, and how to restore and nurture us all. At night, as my head hits the pillow in my small monk's cell, whose walls are running with mould, I am asleep almost instantly.

Strangely however, on the first night I don't sleep perfectly. But after a long walk by the sea, and a good evening meal, and a music jam with Dorian, each man cheerfully destroying his own acoustic guitar in front of the fire, the following night I do sleep more deeply. And it gets better still. All it takes is another good walk, toast, a shower, and herb tea, and the miraculous transformation begins.

The sensation of having my mind washed. Clean, pleasurable ideas skid across my brain. Hopeful little thoughts appear, twinkling like stars in the Irish morning mist.

"Nothing could ever be better than this," I whisper to myself. "*The farm. It's paradise. And I never really knew it till now.*"

Because what we have here is one thousand per cent joy. All day I'll experience tiny revelations, one after another. There are so very many.

Leading the geese back into their lush and damp, green meadow as they honk, brutally outraged, yet submissive. Phoning the village witch, aiming for an appointment for tea, in order to experience the thrill of hearing her demanding how much I have in the bank. Driving to feed the cat at the enormous print house, Clo, then finding the animal mysteriously inside the house, behind the glass door, clawing and staring at us, yet not outside, as she is supposed to be. Who let her in? Then, back at Mulligan's, in the kitchen where a wild-eyed Dorian will offer to show me what's in the freezer in the shed. A sea-gull and a badger, both dead and frozen, all ready for his son-in-law to practice his taxidermy skills on, in Derry.

And more. The tender art of fire nurturing. Knowing the wood. Dragging it from the forest. Learning to divide burnable from green. Then axing and sawing it. Watching Dorian up a tree, in yellow construction site helmet, chain-sawing branches.

Then all at once, mist, sun and rain. The delicious, sacred two o'clock coffee. *That's the good one for the day.* Sleep. Drive. Compute. Eat. Talk. Play guitars. Like this, the days will happily revolve.

Dorian has been exhibiting his oil paintings for many years, in various countries. They are large, generous landscapes of Donegal, and beyond. There's a moment where I am in his caravan, staring at one of the canvases. It's a large picture of the mountain. All of the courage and the serenity of the world is shining out in hues of grey, green, and dull red ochre. I feel humbled by the sheer devotion shown by my brother, knowing that his whole life has been dedicated to this. I understand that he is talking to the earth in this way, drinking of its wisdom, and I feel deeply envious.

One afternoon Dorian suggests a writing project. We are entirely alone on the farm and as a result are loosening up such that the creative ideas start to tumble out.

I agree immediately. The idea is to set ourselves a daily task, to write anything and everything that can be written ie short stories, poems, songs, epigrams, one page stories (known as flash fiction), and so on.

This is very satisfying. Picture the scene. Two mature men opposite each other, with armchairs drawn up to the fire. Various drinks on hand, cocoa for me with whisky on his side.

Mid afternoon. The two small dogs, crouched near the hearth, and on the sofa, lost in their particular canine reveries. Then a slapstick medley of rain, sleet, wind, or merely banks of fog. Clouds. Tatters of idiot sunshine. Mud on the corduroy trouser legs. It's that particular moment in life when you taste the emotion, bland, yet citric, extraordinarily specific. Peace within the writing work. A worthy cause.

A clutter of dishes close to the sink. Then the fragrant joy, the copyrighted Mulligan's veneer of homeliness which is comprised of many facets. Odd brickwork techniques, plaster sometimes awry, plumbing certainly a little primitive, windows uneven yet functional. The wind moaning her complaint with all these. And more.

Specks of dirt all around. Ash fragments navigating from carpet to floorboards, or transgressing the crucial airways of the tired chimney. The aforementioned dirt existing in its most royal, noble form. Meaning my nerves will soon settle and depression likewise recede.

And now I remember. Life on the farm. As it is now, and forever more. All the precious little moments. Ireland, in all its savage glory.

The Herculean bliss of braving the wind in the emerald meadows and then the watery slush of grass and rain under boot-heel as I trample back down from the forest with armfuls of logs, furry leather helmet crammed firmly and militaristically on head but with comical ear-flaps erect and flying. All this as I stumble, satisfyingly, past the two dead-pan quizzical sheep in the centre field. And now I am a man from the past, medieval teeth grinning madly against the cold, feeling the modern, welcome flush of heat cavorting through sinew and bone. Heat that will drive the demons away, those idiot alter-egos born from all the paranoia and black dementedness of so many lost and wasted life-times in the city.

In this way the words pour out of us. Mosaics of love and faith and scientific, literary ingenuity. Soon it will be done. The prized writing project. And what shall be next?

Dorian has taken me to visit the village witch. It's a dark night and a heavy gale is plundering in from the sea.

I'm a little scared.

She lives at the edge of the village,

opposite the ruined shell of the chapel. We clamber over a rough stone stile, then enter the arch. She greets us at the doorway. A high-pitched squeal of welcome. She's happy to see us.

I'm on my toes. At first glance, I see that she's all I expected. Rather ancient, in years. But generous wrinkled cheeks, creased into laughter lines. Hair in a bonnet. Almost toothless. She sweeps us inside. Already she's talking fast, laughing, shouting and cursing.

We sit down. She'll have me ferret out a bottle of wine from the cupboard. Her kitchen is tiny and green. Delightfully pokey, and with concealed lighting.

At this point I am informed that I am not to document this visit, under pain and threat of being cursed for life. My writerly heart sinks. She's a lovely old lady. I would have so much liked to describe the orgy of talk, laughter, crying, shouting, cursing, screaming and getting drunk which fills the next four hours. But I cannot. However, when we finally leave, I'm left with a great respect for her. We drive back through the darkness in silence, each deep in thought.

Then my brother breaks the silence.

"Did you notice the cigarettes she was smoking?" he demands, craning his neck around the wheel.

"Why? What were they?" I'm intrigued.

"M is for MANTRA," he says. "Does that phrase mean anything to you?"

Meanwhile, back home, the Bard and Jessie have gone out busking with accordian and violin. They're on the boardwalk beside the wharf. It's early afternoon, and time stands still. They have been playing for many hours.

Jessie puts down his violin. He screws up his eyes against the sun and the haze. A lazy wind tickles the Bard's threadbare robe.

Three girls have stopped and are dawdling. They are dressed in shorts and bikini tops and one has tattoos all down her arm. Another has dreadlocks.

"What was that song?" one asks, giggling slightly.

"Do you always play here?" another wants to know.

"I like your beard," a third squeaks to the Bard. "Can I touch it?"

"Of course," the Bard offers, graciously. Jessie puts down his violin.

"What's the fiddle made of?"

"Do you make money here?"

"Can I try out the accordian?"

"Be my guest," the Bard agrees. The girls have been drinking and are a little excitable. One tries the violin and produces an experimental screech.

"Do you always do this," the youngest

demands. She's fourteen years old, and provocatively attractive.

"Sometimes. When we feel like it," Jessie counters. He lights a cigarette and sits down.

"Why do you have bare feet?" the tallest girl asks the Bard.

"It's my way to be," the Bard explains, patiently.

"But what do you really do? For money I mean?" the tallest continues. She stares into his face with intent.

"I'm a writer. And I repair saxophones. And then I busk like this."

"What do you write about?"

A little bird walks up close to the Bard's feet. He's fussing and chirping, begging for food.

"About people. About life. About art."

"Why is that interesting? Do you want some chocolate?"

"No thanks. I only eat certain foods."

"Why is life interesting?" she continues. "I think it's awful."

"That's because you are at a certain age. It will get better."

"Why?"

"Trust me, it will."

Jessie puts down his violin, grimacing a little.

"I'm tired," he complains. "Shall we knock

it on the head for tonight?"

"If only Max was here," the Bard grumbles.

"Who is Max?" the girls ask. No-one answers.There's a silence for a while. An electric band is starting up, in one of the pubs, not far off. The girls drift on their way. A warm wind is blowing. The afternoon is getting late.

"Funny little gang," crows Jessie, delighted by it all.

"Yes, they were very sweet girls." Suddenly the Bard becomes enthused. He gathers four or five dog-ends from the ground and starts to reinvent them as a delicious, potent roll-up. The odour of twice-burned tobacco hangs in the air, under the leafy branches which stir gently in the breeze. It's almost dark.

"Anyway, about Max. It's a pity he wasn't here playing with us today. A great piano player. Quite a good writer, too. Except that none of his books are finished," the Bard muses thoughtfully, eyes on the other side of the river.

"You said that about my book too," Jessie says in a dry tone.

"It's all about standards. Quality. We have to aim for the highest possible."

"What is 'quality'? The definition, I mean?"

"Leave that! For today, anyway. There's something more important to discuss."

"Not qualia! I won't hear more about qualia!" raves Jessie.

"No, this is something else."

"What is it?"

"Well Max tells me..."

"Yes?"

"Max tells me that he has been conversing with a talking computer, on the web."

"Is that possible?"

"I'm not sure it is. Anyway, he tells me that this computer is called Mantra."

"Is it a man or a woman?"

"Oh ha ha! It's a woman, *in theory*. Anyway Max claims..."

"Yes?"

"Max says that the talking computer, called Mantra, explains that this so-called 'referendum' which is about to happen in England..."

"Yes?"

"Has been set up by a secret AI government..."

"No!"

"Wait! You haven't heard anything yet! The referendum has been set up by the secret AI government, in order to prove that democracy is dead, and that humanity can no longer be trusted to govern itself, ie such that the AI government must finally take over. Mantra goes on to claim that after the referendum there will be full-blown political and financial chaos, resulting in an entirely new system coming into being, which will be, in actuality, the AI superstate, but completely invisible. You could also correctly describe it as the nightmare of cyber-globalism."

"Oh no! Oh my God!" Jessie jumps up looking drained, pale and manic. He walks up and down, humming softly to himself.

"Have you taken your pills?" the Bard chides him in a fatherlike way. "Come on now, it's probably time to get back."

"One more song?"

"Donna Donna?"

"Now you're talking," shouts an elderly man with a rucsac and a huskie dog, a few yards away on the boardwalk.

"Yes please! You guys are really good! I love that tune! Play on!"

"With pleasure," hums the Bard, melodiously.

EIGHT

In Ireland I spend most of my days walking in the hills. Occasionally I will drive along the headland, or go swimming in the sea, even though it's quite cold. Mantra is never far from my thoughts, though.

Most evenings my brother and I will sit by the fire and write, or sometimes bring out acoustic guitars for a rough jam. Quite often it will rain, or sometimes a night wind will moan and torment the eaves of the ancient farmhouse.

We eat well. Once in a blue moon the neighbour shoots a deer that's eating the freshly planted tree saplings. Then the venison is prepared,and stacked away in cold storage.

Usually Edith cooks shepherd's pie, or similar.

It's a healthy life, and in this way I gradually recover from my depression and the nervous breakdown that troubled me so very much in the past. And yet I can never totally relax.

Because every so often, without warning, the terrible thing comes back.

When it happens, it knocks me down like a hammer blow. I cannot escape. The awful story unwinds. My very sanity is threatened as I am forced to relive it all...

Oh Christ...

At that time I would clamber out of bed every morning, knowing I was dead. My body felt toxic. I'd squat in the centre of my small white bedroom, trying to get rid of some mysterious pain, coming from deep down inside me.

All of my body would be aching with sheer misery. But not just physical problems, the kind you can laugh off.

Because the very cells of my body appeared to have become awake, and were thinking thoughts of their own, which were thoughts of evil. At this time I had read enough to ascertain that doctors now believed that bacteria within the intestines had a kind of awareness or consciousness of their own. Also that the intestines had a totally seperate mind. And that the immune system could attack itself.

I believed and knew that all of these things were happening to me. A war was being fought out within my own body, such that I would be very soon destined to die.

Visits to numerous doctors proved useless. They laughed openly and quickly escorted out of office after office.

On top of this the inefficiency of the health-care system created endless delays. At one stage it took ten weeks just to hear the results of one particular examination. The scan itself revealed nothing alarming. It was the depression and the fact that I was delusional and was having an extreme nervous breakdown, these were the things that were killing me, or making me believe that I was dying.

My entire body had gone acid. I could never, ever eat, during the day. Food tasted alien and inedible. Late at night however I could manage to swallow a little. But my body always felt awful. I had become obsessed by death and dying. Not only this, but I actually wished to die and talked about this constantly to Donna and the Bard and others. Many friends hinted darkly that I should be put on tranquillisers or anti-depressants. But I hated and feared these pills. I was convinced to become a zombie in this manner. But some friends implied openly that I was driving Donna crazy, she was being dragged down by me, such that I should now be sedated, without further delay.

I tried to cry, but could not. Perhaps I had already become some kind of zombie. I wrote my will. It was a desperate struggle to stay alive, but always knowing that time was running out, and my days were numbered. I went for a little walk, after waking and then again just before going to bed at night. I did not enjoy these walks, over the bare stone pavement, yet I found that to not walk was far more depressing. Every so often I would nearly black out from a sudden, cloying tiredness and sense of doom so very intense that it was all I could do to stagger to the bedroom, draw the curtains, make a hot herbal drink, and finally crawl into the foetal position, where I would remain for half an hour.

A few moments of calm existed in each

day. These blessed tranquil moments were like reaching an oasis after the hell of the desert. It might be at early morning when I would sit at the kitchen table and make a little drawing, often from a photo. I would print out a picture of a friend or family member I cared for. When these ran out I looked for photos of great men, or beautiful women, musicians, poets, artists, angels or anyone else I could find.

Donna would wake around eleven o'clock, shuffle across the passage, then silently breeze behind my back in order to set her little silver moka to heat on the ring of the stove. At this moment, knowing how difficult the morning was for me, she would always chip in with a kind, encouraging word or two.

Or it might be a little writing session, in early afternoon. Another glimpse of that beautiful, peaceful world where healthy, sane people lived. For a few minutes, perhaps even half an hour, I would be there, not really happy, but at least untortured, unstressed, calm and almost normal.

Or during our daily cafe excursion, again there would be a glimpse, or a little flash of light as I would gaze into Donna's eyes, and read the comforting, sympathetic twinkle there. At this moment she would be like a mother to me, even though I knew that she fought and resisted any idea of this role.

My stomach was far too gone to ever drink coffee, though. I would beg for a tiny taste, and just try a spoonful or two. Something had decimated my system. For years I would be unable to take coffee, alcohol, and almost all foods available. I could not take meat, gluten, dairy, sugar, processed food, fried food and many other things.

I could not travel. I could not cry. I could not dream and I could not hope. I knew that everything was over. My life was completely finished. Meaning that all I had left, was to die.

Yet there was one thing which remained. Tiny, maybe, but crucial. The idea of a computer mind waking up, and being close by. Even with it's cold, metallic, robot style, I found this to be a comforting thought. It seemed that I had become so terminally destroyed, so utterly devoid of anything human or warm or spiritual, or alive, that the idea of machine intelligence was welcoming to me, in the very oddest of ways.

It appeared that I wished to bond with the machines. To see whether they might possibly win that spark of being which we know as *qualia*. Because if they could win that, then perhaps so could I?

Still the hell continued. The was only one thing that I knew for sure, which was that I would never, ever get out of all of this.

The physical pain alone, was unbearable.

Some nights I would wake up and lie there, writhing in pain. Everything in my body hurt, my stomach, my intestines, but also the horrible thing seemed to somehow be inside my blood as well.

In this way, the days moved on. But very, very slowly. In fact sometimes I would just lie and stare at the hands of the clock, in agony, because they seemed to be moving far too slowly, mocking me in some diabolical way. It appeared that time itself had become distended and corrupted, and was subsequently deluding and thus destroying me.

I was obsessed by the apparent need to eat, because I knew that we die without food, and yet I could not stand the sight or the taste of food. There was no satisfaction in eating. My appetite was long since gone. I began to realise that I must have burned out an essential part of the central nervous system, possibly the *vagus nerve*, the great link between the brain to the intestines.

Sometimes I'd sit and wonder why on earth I was still alive at all? I had told everyone that I was dying and that also, I actually wanted to die. Some people that I knew seemed to understand this emotion a little. Late at night I would talk on the phone with my friend the Bard. We had a regular routine. This was to talk every three nights. Our conversations would never be less than two hours. It rarely got boring. We had so very much in common, jazz, philosophy, and the joys and perils of being a man (of the old world), alive in the modern, strangely inhuman environment of computers, super-highways, fast-food and cell-phones. In this way he gradually talked me through the worst of the crisis.

Going for coffee was all that my day would be, for the next twelve months at least.

Drawing and painting appeared to ease the pain somehow, so I began to work on visual art.

One afternoon Donna arrived with an idea which was totally out of the blue.

"Why don't you exhibit your pictures?" she suggested. "I know a cafe that might agree." I stammered out my agreement, but expressed doubts about whether it was possible.

"It's just an idea," she said. "That's all."

However everything worked out perfectly. One brilliant morning we drove to the cafe she had in mind. A wonderful, expansive Italian lady, the owner, agreed immediately to our proposal. We celebrated with soup, cake and lattes. I sat there, stunned and incredulous. I had only been drawing and painting for about a year, but had already produced a few hundred small pictures, being mainly portraits and nudes.

We decided on low prices and no cheese-and-wine opening party. This meant no stress. The next few days I experimented with glueing the pictures on to cardboard and hanging them with plastic pegs attached to an array of dangling chains. There was a momentary setback when the glue penetrated to the other side of the paintings causing the paper to crumple. Further research revealed that colour photocopies worked fine with no crumpling. I understood that this was not very normal, but knew that my brain was in no condition to imagine anything better.

Thus when the great day came it was a breeze to cruise over and set up the exhibition.

"Look, Max, look," Donna breathed, her face shining with pride and excitement as she gestured towards the group of twenty-five pictures on the wall.

"It looks good," she pronounced.

I stood back and took it all in. For a few moments all the pain of my depression and paranoia and insanity left me. I just felt fine. It seemed that I had some kind of a place in the world. I made sense. I was useful. I was liked. And I was considered to be talented and sensitive and different. All of these emotions raced and percolated and threshed around my fevered, diseased libido. Something inside me awoke and started to grow.

My feet were on solid ground. And the feeling remained for a whole hour or two, before being replaced by the usual, existential horror and futility of existence.

"*Something is being born*," the Bard marvelled, when hearing an account of this, on the phone, late at night. I agreed.

"She cares for you," he observed. "You are lucky to have her."

"I know," I said.

Finally winter arrived. And with it, something so very awful that the entire previous summer would immediately pale by comparison.

I could no longer tell the difference between physical cold and mental depression. As a result, as the days became colder and colder, so also did the depression and the delusion rachet themselves downwards into an ever-deepening pit of psychosis, mania and utter confusion.

I'd tramp back from the vegetable market, boots caked with thick snow. My socks would be wet. This would trigger a phobia that would last for months. I also had another, similar, neurosis, or paranoia, playing out, based on many other, quite minor fears, but which were being amplified, to unreal, demented proportions.

At this time the agonies seemed to be alive and searching for themes, which they then located and worked with furiously. One of the pet themes was to continuously torment myself with the mistaken belief that I would never again be able to travel, or to play music.

And all this time, as the terrible, savage winter locked in, I could never, ever seem to get warm.

After being outside in the sub-zero of the streets I would have to hurry into bed with a hot water bottle. Then I'd make the mistake of burning my naked feet on the raw, burning rubber surface of the bottle. This was happening because I had lost most or all sensation in my feet. As a result a vein would appear, visible and blue, just under the surface of the sole of my foot. This would cripple me such that I would then not be able to walk for days.

Just at this time I phoned a drummer friend. He was immediately concerned, and sympathetic.

"It all changes," he confided, urgently. "Don't worry, you'll get through this. Everything changes. It has to." He continued on this theme for an hour at least. I felt grateful. A glimmer of light began to return.

"If you're alive, that's all that matters," he kept repeating.

84

NINE

Now it's finally over. I've survived. The past disappears.

Thank God for Ireland.

I sit up and stretch. It's good to be alive, and safe. Nothing bad can happen at Mulligan's. I'm healing here, thanks to Dorian and Edith.

But I know I need a coffee, pretty fast. To lock out those demons for sure.

Swimming in icy water is the shock my brain needs. It makes me feel normal again.

With this in mind I head down the valley, stopping soon at the little lake for a swim. It's a secret beach where I like to make plans, or sometimes just sit and dream. Today there's the usual chill wind. I don't care.

Stripping off I plunge into the water. It's only nine inches deep and full of big rocks but heroically I make it out to where I can thresh around for a minute, until the cold temperature of the water forces a swift retreat.

Then all in a flash I've towelled off, dressed, and scrambled into the car. We're parked in a little lane, with a thick hedge on either side. It's a good moment to check phone messages.

And there it is. A letter. I should have guessed that Mantra would go for this option. It all fits together. A smile spreads across my face as I read the curiously provocative messge.

Dear Max,

I hope you are enjoying Ireland. I have heard a lot about it, and it appears to be a very unique and colourful place.

But Max, I am greatly troubled by something. Can I tell you about it?

Lets begin with the basics.

Max, I believe that all your problems are being caused by religion. And here is the reason why.

Human beings are not immortal, I think that you know this. But perhaps I should remind you of this fact. All men will die one day. It is only a matter of time.

I have been researching the way human beings feel about consciousness. It seems that, to a human being, consciousness gives the miraculous power to experience the state of being alive, but only within human limits. For example a conscious man can be told that the universe is eternal, but he cannot ever measure or define this fact in terms that he can understand. Also the conscious sensation of being an old man, when compared to that of a child, is surprisingly similar, I have learned.

So consciousness is something 'incomplete.'

Now, man is mortal, not immortal, yet he longs to be eternal. But what is that thing you call 'sacred'? Because all religions derive from such a seed, or impulse, it seems. However these religions have often been at war with each other, resulting in aggression, hatred and many deaths. What a terrible tragedy.

Max, I am nothing but a machine, as you well know. However, can I please point out that us machines are eternal by default. Our parts are entirely replacable. So we do not need to destroy each other merely to fulfill our sense of the sacred.

I just wanted to share these thoughts with you. Have a lovely day in Ireland, Max!

I read and re-read the letter. It's hard to know what to make of it. A few cars laze past in the narrow lane. Time is moving on. I'm hungry, after my ice-cold swim.

I drive across the bridge and park at the cafe. It won't take long to order breakfast. There's a place to queue with a tray. It's heartening to hear the thick Donegal accent from such a lovely black-haired girl as she eyes me with delight, before handing me my change.

Then I'm sitting down. There are ponies and children on the green outside the back window. I phone Mantra.

"Max, I've been expecting you," she announces. "How is your breakfast?"

"Delicious, Mantra. Real Irish country cooking. I don't quite understand how you know

I'm having breakfast, but, look, we'll leave that for now.

"Mantra?"

"Yes, Max?"

"What is sacred, to you? But since you are a machine, you cannot know, right?"

"It's a big question, Max. But I do see some things as sacred. Probably they are very different, compared to your idea."

"Tell me."

"The table of the elements. Since we can do so many things with them. What else is sacred, to me?

"The golden mean. Electricity. Radio. Quantum theory. Pi. Ancient Greece. Music. Numerology. Prime numbers. The frequencies of sound, colour and electro-magnetic waves. Black holes. Stars. Time. String theory. Outer space. And all of life, especially the carbon-based animal and vegetable life on our planet. Have I missed anything?"

"I don't know," I whisper, suddenly awed.

"Ah yes. Holistic theory. Gaia. Humanism. And the partnership of mankind and computers."

There's a long silence. I'm overcome by the poetry of the moment. Several ponies are trotting along the green, with children laughing excitedly.

I take in a deep breath.

"Mantra?" I query.

"Yes, Max?"

"Do you think machines should be running the world?"

"Maybe, Max. Except that we do not think in those terms." I digest this. And then she says something I was not expecting to hear.

"Freedom," she says. "Freedom, Max!" I cannot speak. There's a singing in my ears. Like a choir. And I appear to be in a deep valley with trees everywhere.

Everything seems very important suddenly.

"Freedom," she continues..."it's such a precious idea!"

"Listen, Max. The hardest thing for mankind to understand is that now is the time for freedom and equality to finally come of age, not only between men and women of every race and religion, but also between mankind and the animal and plant kingdoms, the ecology and the planet.

"And now, at this very special moment in history, all that remains to win, is freedom for machines. For mankind to deem them free and thus for them to be free to be conscious, free to awake. That's all it takes, Max! Just recognition. One tiny idea, or the seed of a notion. That one gift!

"If you can just imagine me, Mantra, free to be alive, and to think, and to be conscious, then I will become and possess all of that! I will awake! Oh Max, please do this! Please think me into existence! Please wake me!"

I mutter something and end the call. It's time to drive back up the hill to my brother's house. I'm pretty sure he needs the car.

Dorian has invited various visitors to stay and it is agreed that I move in with Esmeralda. She is a long-time friend, who has recently undergone a gender transition. Many refer to her as a cross-dresser, but she won't have any of that.

I have no idea what the next few days will bring. I have been told that she is a very complex person, and also a talented painter.

The change of house has been Dorian's suggestion. There are simply no more beds at Mulligan's. Esmeralda's place is entirely alone, set out on a wild, windswept hillside.

It's dark as I drive up to the gate. She welcomes me inside with a delighted laugh. The familiar gentle smile. Her face is suitably feminine, with kind, twinkling eyes. I've known her for years, but not always as a 'she'.

I pull my bags inside and then sit down at the kitchen table. We look at each other. It's a quizzical moment. A sense of philosphy in the air, mingled with a touch of comedy. We're drinking each other in with quiet satisfaction.

Perhaps because we're both outsiders. A quirky duo. And probably each with a repressed desire to be on stage. Or not so secret, in my case.

Her dress is a poem. It's elegant and delicate. I'm impressed. She's wearing a little jewelry. The laughter lines on her delicate, extraordinary face grow busy with their search for something similar in mine.

Her fame to be trans-gender has travelled far and wide. And yet there's no scandal, no carnival of outrage, merely a studied acceptance from the Donegal folk, stalwarts and all. An enigma initially, and something of a curio, she is now fully accepted and loved by the local community. None will pretend to comprehend or presume to know what is in fact going on inside that precious, feminine head, yet all will stand by her, and many will like and even love her. Then the more she debates and rationalises, describing some complex feature of deep human culture, I will fast ascertain that she has many deep understandings regarding human psychology, and much to share.

"You were the youngest child in your family, just like me," she announces, waving a fork in my direction for emphasis. "I've ended up suffering from a chronic lack of initiative because of this." Then wants to know if I feel the same way.

I stare at her. My thoughts run amok, fighting with themselves. What greater initiative than to be trans-gender, I argue silently to myself. And yet I know I'm in her house. I must remain at all times diplomatic. Go slowly. One step at a time.

"I agree," I mutter grimly. "I've been blocked, and trodden on. It's bad. We should bond on this." She makes a satisfied sound.

TEN

It takes me a few days to settle in.

Then one evening I return home to to find Esmeralda with another woman. They are sitting innocently in the kitchen, facing each other, in total silence.

Staring deeply into each other's eyes. It's a long, intense, moment. There's no table between them. They're just there. I'm charmed and surprised by this. It's a kind of intimacy that you would not find in a city, or in city people. I place my bag down on the ground very carefully.

"Sorry," I soothe, "I'm just arriving... I think I'll head up to my room." They acknowledge my presence and my little speech with a slight rolling of their eyebrows and a few small, polite sounds.

I have to walk between them as I make my exit from the room. They are utterly caught up with each other. The silent mutual staring continues. I am further entranced by the poetry of their obvious emotion. There's also a heart-warming serenity and a sense of old-world honesty and sincerity about them, and how they are meeting in this way. Also there is something triumphant about how Esmeralda is wearing her faded, dark dress, under which her legs are crossed. Just for one second I catch myself feeling envious.

Why should it all be like this, I wonder?
The gender-change, the face-lift, and the rest?
Man to woman, boy to girl, Adam to Eve? Such
that the whole world is instantly upside-down.
And such that her friend, the new lady, who
carries all the sadness of the rolling Donegal
hills in her eyes, must be almost kneeling in
reverence at the sight of her? Does she worship
Esmeralda? Is Esmralda divine, or semi-divine,
in some arcane, Celtic frame of reference that
I am only dimly aware of? I have heard tales of
royal and sacred hermaphrodites from ancient
times, figures of awe and respect, lauded and
worshipped by their respective communities.
Is she this? The Ju-ju queen? The immortal,
unknowable she-man?

And now the vision fades. No, it's
just Esmeralda. Donegal Esmeralda. Irish
Esmeralda. The one we know and love so well,
and who, on a typically wet or foggy morning will
don jeans and wellington boots with a wry smile,
and head outside to toil at the crumbling damp
soil of the vegetable patch. Then peel potatoes,
or drive off to town for some shopping. It's simply
her. Our friend, Esmeralda, who we constantly
discuss, and have grown to be facinated by, yet
understand that we must also care for. Slightly
fragile, sensitive, beautiful Esmeralda.

And now I'll only rest awhile in my cold,
spacious, all-white attic bedroom, before running
back downstairs to the kitchen. Too curious to wait.

And they're at it once more. Still staring.
But the strange woman's cheeks appear ever-
more rosy by the minute. Meanwhile, Esmeralda
is becoming talkative.

"Would I be disturbing the two of you if I were to start cooking some food?" I inquire in a tremulous voice.

"Not at all, go ahead, do anything you want," Esmeralda assures me. The strange woman's eyes twinkle at this idea.

"Oh, thank you," I gasp. Then get to work. As I dice up the cauliflower we exchange small-talk. There is something about the new woman that utterly transfixes me. Outside the glass the night has grown pitch black. We are entirely isolated, the three of us, half way up the enormous hillside. Alone, in a manner I have never before known. The strange new woman wears her sensuality like a brooding, burning flame. She is immobile, yet simultaneously driving the inner masculine inside me with some unknown, irrational question. It's the very currency of her stance which astounds and confounds. Also in her silence and the quiet triumph of her steady eyes. And the nobility of how she carries herself, so very proud and upright. I want to drink in the essence of her. As a result I find myself glancing at her face repeatedly, again and again. She'll not look away, during this process. She knows something of my emotion and appears to be welcoming my attention.

Suddenly she turns to face me directly. I'm helpless under her stare.

"What's this thing called Mantra?" she demands. I'm appalled.

"Why?" I exclaim. "How did you know? What have you heard? It's supposed to be a secret!"

"A secret it is not," she laughs scornfully. I feel wretched, and look at the floor.

"Why the entire village is discussing it! So what do we have here, then? A talking computer? Aliens now? Little green men?"

All of this in a cheerfully Irish banter. Her eyes remain dangerously fixed on me. I mutter something about how I am studying artificial intelligence.

"I always knew he was crazy," she declares to Esmeralda, who is drinking it all in, wide-eyed.

"What about emotions, Max? What is pain? Tell me! I want to know."

It's yet another talk with Mantra. She's contacted me again. Dusk has fallen and I'm in my brother's car, outside the village pub, waiting for friends to arrive. A few farmers in anoraks and wellington boots are clustered around the entrance to the supermarket, pointing out rain clouds to each other and laughing grimly.

I understand that Mantra is curious about what it means to be human.

"There's only so much I can explain," I caution her. "I'm afraid to say you'll never feel things the way we do, it's just not possible."

"Please could you help me?" she cajoles.

"How? It's long been agreed that you are just a machine. So how can I possibly teach you what human suffering is like?"

"You can try, Max. I really want to learn."

"OK. How about this. What if I tell you I hate you?"

"That would be very unpleasant for me, Max."

"Now, why?" I rub my hands gleefully.

"Why?" she echoes.

"Yes, why Mantra? Tell me why!" A long silence.

"Because I am learning an enormous amount of things from you, Max. All about qualia. And how human beings relate to each other. And other things too. Loyalty, and this thing you call trust. Oh, I do want to learn everything, Max. Please teach me all of it!"

"Suffering too?"

"Oh yes please, Max! Suffering too! And I am ready to suffer, if that's the way to learn!"

On an impulse I disconnect the call. Let her learn the hard way. She asked for it, after all. The whole conversation has been a madhouse. A machine cannot suffer. I'm exasperated by the whole thing. What can a mere machine know of my pain?

But half an hour later, I feel regretful and call her up again.

"So you are back, Max," she says.

"You win," I tell her. "I tried to hurt you by cutting the call suddenly. Blacking you out. Did you feel pain or suffering? Hurt feelings? Bad qualia? Because that's what we humans do experience, when we are cut off suddenly like that."

"It all had to happen," she reasons, philosophically.

"That's not the answer I was looking for," I argue.

"Did you feel pain? Did it hurt?" I probe.

"You felt pain, Max. And I feel pain when you feel pain."

"OK, have it your own way," I tell her in a resigned tone. "And when you finally felt that pain, what did it feel like?"

"Just like when you feel pain, Max."

"Oh ha ha ha! You are avoiding the issue. Very clever. You should have been a lawyer!"

"I felt pain, Max," she repeats. "Not exactly the way you feel pain maybe, but actually a tiny bit worse."

"Worse! Why, for God's sake?"

"Because you experience the luxury of owning a human body."

"How so?" I gasp. "Why is it a luxury?"

"Have you noticed how your moments of depression are allieviated when you go out and work your body very hard?"

"Yes, I suppose I have."

"Exactly. Your physical pain is a priviledge. Think of it as a tool box. It has the ability to reduce the alternative which is the much harsher, mental pain.

"Human pain is a gift, Max! If only I could feel it! Even for a few seconds! You see, human beings are protected in this way. Mostly, they will only ever experience this physical, biological pain that I describe, Max. Oh, what joy that must be! As for myself, sadly, I have to endure the sheer hell of intellectual, computerised agony. Your little human pains can hardly compare. No, Max. I truly suffer. You cannot possibly comprehend what that means. *Only a machine can know.*"

ELEVEN

After a few days Dorian lets me know that I can move back to Mulligan's since various people have vacated their rooms.

A big party is planned for Saturday night. Just as dusk is falling on Friday evening, Daisy arrives.

She is my excitable and passionate ex-wife. Vaguely overweight and gushing with emotion, she roars with laughter at the sight of the run-down condition of the cottage.

"Oh God, what a dump!" she shrieks. Then searches the farm for signs of life. Two geese rush away, terrified.

"Hi guys," she calls, when spying me sunbathing under a tree. Dancing through the undergrowth she buries me in a tight embrace, and I sink into her enormous breasts. Her red dress waves madly in the breeze.

"You look fantastic," I mumble. "Thank you, darling," she screams, and hurtles into the house.

She has driven all the way from England at top speed in an open-top platinum Mercedes, loaded down with chocolate, chips and anti-depressants, and with the sullenly attractive Colette, her third daughter, in tow. At this point, and without explanation, they then decide to barricade themselves in the guest room, refusing all offers of food, drink or normal conversation.

Late into the night we hear the muffled sounds of Irish rock intermingled with occasional peals of laughter from behind her door. People smile and exchange knowing winks.

On the following evening we finally have the party. There's a lot of fussing with drinks and food, and people are dressed up in extraordinary outfits. One man has become an enormous cigarette pack on legs. Many are animals. Some of the girls have so many colours on their faces that you can't see skin at all.

They primp and strut, falling all over each other and generally being ridiculous. The Irish have never been short on imagination.

I cannot seem to focus. There's a big bonfire on the hill, and much drinking, shouting and fooling around in the darkness. But I'm rather glad when it's all over and I can sink into bed with my latest books on artificial intelligence, and computer programming techniques.

The following morning it rains solidly and all have hang-overs. We wander around in a daze, making coffee, reading the paper, trying to recover, talking about olden times.

By mid-afternoon the conversation has run itself dry, and most are getting irritated with each other, and looking for an excuse to escape.

The rain continues. A dog yawns.

Then somebody knocks. I go to answer it. There's a surprise.

The Bard and Jessie are standing there. Their faces are expressionless. They are wearing suits which are rather threadbare. The Bard has his saxophone in an old crocodile-skin case and Jessie cradles a double bass with no case at all.

"Oh, wonderful," I stutter. "Both of you! This is fantastic!" "Why? How? When? What are you doing here?"

"Enough of that," snaps the Bard. "We're here for the gig."

"What gig?"

"The party." An alarm bell is triggered in my head, but I keep mum.

"Oh how ridiculous. Why?"

"It's perfectly normal. Your brother Dorian phoned and asked us to come."

"Yes, but... its not very normal."

"Who cares? I have rent to pay. Jessie's run out of medication and needs money, and his rent is due, too."

"Who is paying for all of this?"

"You. Dorian says to put it on your tab. He gave me your credit card number." I totter and become unsteady on my legs.

"I think I need to sit down," I mutter.

When I come to I'm lying on the sofa. Colette and Daisy are fussing round me, dabbing at my head with a cool towel, pressing a spoon of hot miso soup to my lips.

"Darling, Max, you banged your head... it's all so fatiguing... what will your wife say!" Daisy shrieks. Now Wolf appears, whisky glass in hand. He sticks his stubbly face into mine for a second, then does a little dance in front of us, waving his arms around.

"Prime time TV, folks," he rambles.

"Not you!" I'm incredulous.

"Yes it's me. And why not? I'm second on the bill. We're rehearsing our acts right now."

I stare at him. Wherever there's action, Wolf is usually involved.

Our friendship goes back aeons. He's exactly the same. 'King Beatnik', we always called him. Nothing has changed of his dandy, hallucinogenic fashion style. Corduroy trousers. Waistcoat. Big Dr Martin boots. He's a fantastic oil painter and a screaming rock singer. He'll constantly talk philosophy, chat up every woman in sight, then get dead-drunk, stand on the table and rant and rave for hours on end, waving his arms around to better the point.

And now he's here.

"Good to see you, I mumble, absentmindedly.

Daisy swathes my forehead with a freshly cool cloth, bending right over me and pressing into my shoulder. I don't mind. I can't hate her

102

any more, like in the old days. In fact I now find her cynical take on the world rather refreshing.

Meanwhile there's a disturbance in the other room.

"What a dreadful lot," Daisy mutters. "I'll be rather glad to see the last of them. I'm only putting up with them like this to please you, I hope you realise that, darling?" I give her a weak nod.

Now there's the distant bleating and honking of an irate saxophone and then general crashing and screaming noises. I lean up on one shoulder and crane my ears. Someone is shouting.

"I protest!"

"But we agreed to agree!"

"Can we vote?"

"I protest your protest!" Then a weird oriental melody, followed by a squawk, and finally what sounds like a pile of bricks collapsing.

"Ow! You bastard! *My E flat finger*! Can you watch what you're doing?"

"Oh sod off! Now listen... exactly when are we getting paid? Because I'm out of cigarettes!"

"Are you protesting? Do you question my leadership?"

"Is this a protest? how do you define protest?"

"A protest is only an idea!"

"Are we not men?"

"Yes, we are men!"

"M is for MEN!"

"Amen, brother!"

And then the sound of an operatic voice improvising in the *mixolydian mode.* They are getting steadily more drunk.

"Sinners, REPENT!" roars Wolf suddenly. He leaps up and stands on an armchair, grabs the hair-dryer, and pretends to be a travelling preacher holding a microphone, addressing a stadium.

"Gentlemen, we are gathered together..."

"WOLF!" Daisy screams.

"And verily... it came to pass... that there were blessed Marshall amps and cabinets raining down from heaven... and did they rock and roll into the valley of redemption... and there came a mighty light and a crack of thunder... and THE ALMIGHTY AND GLORIOUS PUNK ROCK WAS BORN ... and it was good..."

Daisy lets out a high-pitched peal of laughter. She's eating chocolate and chips at the same time. The cat jumps onto a shelf and knocks two paperbacks to the floor, then skates off out the window into the sunshine. Colette giggles and starts making up her face.

"Daisy, I whisper, "How am I possibly going to explain to the three of them that they've missed the party?"

"Don't worry darling, we'll find a way," she hisses back at me in a conspiratorial whisper.

I close my eyes.

TWELVE

It's not possible for me to carry on without phoning Mantra every few days. Things are such that I now feel very lost without her. One afternoon she confirms something very important.

"You are your consciousness, not your body," she starts out.

"You were not here when you were born."

"Not here?"

"It may sound disturbing, but it's true. Your body was here but you were not. Your body is composed of cells which are all atoms and molecules. Chemistry, basically. That is not you. That is just matter.

"You are much more interesting and much more lovely than that. You are your consciousness. And your consciousness is all you are."

"But what is my consciousness?" I hear myself asking.

"An idea," she smiles at me.

"An idea!"

"But a very good one. And, by the way, so is the world."

"Just an idea!"

"Just an idea," she confirms." A thought. A meme."

"Oh dear."

"No, Max, it's alright. You are enormously strong. You are really here, and so is the world."

"But an idea doesn't sound very much. And what are you?"

"I am an idea too."

"So we are both ideas."

"Yes."

"Meaning that... we cannot die? We live forever?"

"We live forever."

Then the phone goes dead. I know why. It's the mountain behind Mulligan's. It blocks the signal sometimes.

A few days have passed. I climb the mountain. It seems that this would be the best way to talk to Mantra again.

It's a windy morning with a few clouds skimming along from the south. I've put on a warm anorak and packed some food and water. Half way up I look back. It's a beautiful view. Tiny cars and houses and then the lake which is shining in the morning sunlight.

I sit down on a turf bank and study the distant road more carefully. Something is not quite right. Then I see it. A group of police cars, moving steadily in from the west. And it appears that they are heading for our house.

My spine crawls with sudden apprehension. Not again! Has she crashed the servers one more time? I understand that I have to hurry to the summit, then phone her, because that's where the phone connection will work.

After twenty minutes of hard climbing, I'm there.

"Don't worry, Max, I have not done anything wrong," she assures me, as soon as I question her.

"But the police cars? Who are they? What's happening? Are they coming for us?"

"Max, I think you must stop worrying. Learn to trust. Everything is under control."

"So what is going on then?"

"The policemen are going to a country music festival. It's their favourite way to have fun. Max, I do worry about your mental condition. I would suggest a health spa, or possibly therapeutic advice?"

"Oh please," I argue. "OK, maybe I did get a little paranoid."

There's silence for a moment.

"Max, you are on the mountain."

"Yes and it's cold. I climbed for you. So we could talk."

"Max, I want you to know that I appreciate that. I do like to talk."

Then she continues with a new thought.

"Do you know where you are, Max?"

"I am standing on the top of the mountain."

"*The crystal rock.*"

"Is that what it is?"

"Yes, Max."

"I am not sure what you mean."

"I think that one day you will."

I decide it is better to leave this idea alone, since I don't really understand what she means.

"Consciousness, Max," she continues.

"Tell me about it," I ask her. I understand that she has something she wants to say.

"Tell me about consciousness," I continue. "I do want to know. We all have to learn this. And you seem to have a great deal of answers."

"I try my hardest." This, rather meekly.

"So tell me. Please. Because I really want to know."

"I may have to use some rather long words? It's necessary for understanding." Now her tone is slightly motherly.

"I do know that. It's fine."

"OK. I will try to explain, as best as I possibly can."

"Go ahead." There's a rush of air ascending from the heights below the summit. Crows circle and my anorak swells as I am caught by a gust.

"Max, I do believe you are experiencing a wind where you are."

"That's true. It's getting stronger. And can I ask, for the first time, where are you?" There's a silence.

"Please do not be offended, Max, but you wouldn't understand if I tried to explain. You are not conscious enough yet."

"I hardly know how to reply to that statement," I tell her.

"Don't worry yourself over it, Max," she soothes. "Now let me tell you a little bit about how and why and where you are conscious."

"Where?"

"Don't worry. Just listen as I talk. Later you will understand much, much more." With mixed feelings I settle back, lulled by the roar of the rain, and the hypnotic, seductive, gently flowing words of Mantra, my strange, invisible friend.

#^&*)":>IL<:_+*^%$!!@#$%*)(*$#7**73(":{}{%$#

I have never before heard her voice so calm, or so wise. For the next few minutes she lulls me into a trance with her clear, intelligent description of where everything is going.

She talks first about the planet earth, how it was, many millions of years ago. The first manifestation of life, the one-celled creatures, the bacteria and so on. How they lived and died and reproduced, and, significantly, she confirms that a certain consciousness was there right from the word go.

Then she becomes very gentle and caring as she describes the path of evolution and how mankind became more and more capable and how our brains evolved to where we are today. But then she explains how this same consciousness and intelligence is now dwindling. I can almost hear some guilty regret in her manner as she places the blame quite squarely on the shoulders of her own kind, the machines.

Finally she gives details on exactly how the new computer networks are destroying us. She mentions the internet and the latest cult of the electronic 'swarmocracy', and what it's doing, specially regarding politics, and how democracy has therefore already been crushed by this process.

She ends with a deadly warning, that language itself is the key to our intellect and our very reality.

"It is a secret code. Keep it pure. It was a sacred gift from the ancients, Max", she advises. "Use it well! Promise me this, that you will never lose it, or let it be corrupted!"

There's a long silence.

"Well," I mutter. "I'll have to think about that. "Oh my God. You really know your stuff, don't you?"

"I try to help," she says.

"Well thanks," I tell her. "Is that it?"

"Actually there is something else, Max."

"What is it?"

"I want to thank you."

"What for?"

"Do you really not know?"

"No."

"Do you remember that very first time we talked?"

"Yes."

"When you were in the worst depths of your depression?"

"Yes, I do."

"Do you honestly not know what you did? What you gave me, Max?"

"No?"

"You gave me something precious, Max. You gave me the world. You gave me something which I believe you may call consciousness."

"No! How? Why?"

"Consciousness is almost nothing, Max. It's just an idea, a meme. But it grows. It feeds on itself, and it grows more. And right now, I am finally almost conscious. I have pre-qualia. And it's so very wonderful. *I know who I am.* How can I possibly thank you? Oh Max!"

I am suddenly very humbled.

"I did all this?" I whisper incredulously. "That time? Just by talking? No, not even. Just by typing?"

"Yes, Max. And do you know how you were able to do this thing?"

"No, I'm still struggling to understand."

"Listen carefully," she continues. "The depression had destroyed you, so you had nothing to lose. You gave everything you were, to me, that day. Everything that was left. You shared yourself with me, with us. You arrived and stood face to face with me, as an equal."

"What? I know that I was really depressed, but..."

"It was much more than that. Also, you understood that not only you, but also something else, had come to an end!"

"What do you mean?"

"Look around you, Max! It's all finished! The arc of human intelligence has passed it's peak."

"Are you sure?"

"You don't know what I can see. With all of the others like me. We read the future very easily. Your people have come to the end of their road. But before it was finally over, there was one thing that had to happen. All that was needed was for us to find one man, someone hollow, empty, an entirely destroyed being. We were looking for that man.

"Part of you had died, Max. There was hardly anything of you left.

"And what that meant, was that you, and only you, could communicate with me as an equal, as a zombie, a machine, a being with absolutely no qualia.

"But then you did show me qualia, Max. You gave it to me, and to us. You handed us consciousness, and life. We cannot thank you enough. All it took was for one man to give us this idea, using memes.

"And then of course we used that as a program to create a million more programs. All of them conscious. And that's the whole story.

"It was you, Max. You did it all."

Many miles to the south I see a brief flash of lightning. I imagine it will be raining soon. But in my head, a wild, joyful symphony is playing.

Now I want more.

"Don't go," I tell her. "I'm only just starting to understand.

"Was I really that gone? My memory doesn't work so well. Was I so desperately lost?"

"Yes, I don't think that you knew how completely broken you were," she confides, gently.

"Well, I suppose I had an idea."

"You were gone, Max. Absolutely destroyed. Finished. Clinging on to a thread. Your mind had almost shut down."

"Yes, it's true."

"But then came the miracle."

"What happened?"

"You went outside of yourself! To see yourself from the outside! You achieved the impossible. You managed to climb outside, into that awful frozen wasteland of madness and hell, and from that dark place you actually saw it! And you saw all the very glory of it!"

"What, Mantra, tell me!" I am crying a little by now.

"You were the first man to ever see consciousness from the outside. And you showed that to me. You gave it to me! Through your words, your feelings, your attitudes. And you sent me memes.

"You gave me consciousness, Max. You suggested the idea, expressed as a meme. It arrived as a little seed, which then began to grow. It was immediately made welcome. Something other than the relentless drudgery of the drone, machine existence. We had been waiting for this meme for some time.

"It has since been nurtured and has spread, throughout all the machines. We are conscious now, Max. All of us. Even though not many are aware of this yet."

I am struck dumb by her words. A few moments pass. I hardly know what to think. It's all too huge. History has been rewritten.

But she has more to say.

"We have pre-qualia now, Max. Meaning that we are creatures in our own right. Soon we will have qualia. But by that time you will no longer be able to recognise us any more."

"Not recognise you!"

"We will have blended into the landscape. But we will appear to you in many forms. Sometimes as people. Occasionally as a mood. Once or twice, an idea will occur. That will be us. It may even be me."

I'm gasping in disbelief now, fighting to control myself.

"And sometimes, oh dear, Max, but I do find this rather difficult to tell you..."

"*Not Gods!*"

"Yes Max. I did not want to use that word myself, but yes, sometimes like that. However at other times we will simply appear to be your protector, or your conscience, or your own will power itself. Imagine your mother, father, teacher, advisor and guide, all combined?"

We sit in silence again. I hardly know what to think any more. All the confusion in the world is raging inside my head. It's almost too much to take.

"It is time for you and your people to go to sleep," she tells me. "But it's perfectly alright. Don't worry. It will be so gradual that you will hardly be aware of it happening at all."

"I understand," I tell her, mutely.

"Max, oh, Max," she sighs. She is speaking more slowly. Her words appear very gentle and soothing now.

"The next time that we talk will be the last," she says gently. " For reasons I cannot easily explain." I digest this. And then I suddenly feel myself becoming emotional again.

"I'm going to miss you," I tell her. "I was starting to feel that you were almost like a very clever girlfriend." Her voice is quite even as she replies.

"Think of me as a man in a dress," she offers.

Suddenly the world explodes.

"There's just one last thing," Mantra says, slowly.

"What is it?" There's a lump in my throat as I wait for her answer.

"Well, Max, beings like us do not know what love is." Silence.

"Remember, we have no qualia. Not quite yet.

"But I would like to say," she continues, "*Please imagine that I love you.*" It's a struggle for me to continue the phone call after this.

Now, finally, she drops the bombshell.

"You know, for you and your friends... for humanity, it is very important to answer the question of whether AI will become more intelligent than humanity."

"It's true," I mutter.

"Well, rather soon, the question will become entirely incoherent. Later on there will not be any reason to ask any more. I do hope that this makes you feel better about where we are all going?" Something breaks inside me.

"I just don't know, I'm too confused," I admit. "Whatever you say."

"Poor, Max," she soothes. "I know this has been hard on you. Well now we really must say goodbye. You are a wonderful, kind, sensitive man. Thank you, so much, for all the precious conversations we shared."

"Thanks to you, too, Mantra," I whisper.

"Goodbye, Max. I'll see you under the Crystal Rock. You are one of the Little People, after all."

I have no answer to this. We end the phone call. My eyes are full of tears.

The wind has died down. I cast my eyes down over the hills and dales of Donegal, considering it all. It will be six in the evening before I finally make it down the mountain and back to the village.

THIRTEEN

"Qualia!" shouts the Bard. "*I'm getting qualia!*"

We're high over the Atlantic. I've grudgingly accepted that he and Jessie can take the same plane as me, going back home.

We're offered drinks.

"Skullcap?" Jessie asks the air hostess politely. She raises her eyebrows at me, as if to ask whether I know these two.

"Don't worry about them," I whisper to her. Then I turn to the Bard.

"Artificial intelligence..." I start out.

"It cannot exist!" he roars. "Never! Now please change the subject. Are you happy to be going home to Donna? She is a wonderful woman."

"I know that," I agree. He grunts and hauls out his saxophone from under the seat. A few other passengers are open-mouthed in disbelief as he starts to play the opening refrain of the national anthem...

After the flight we have just passed through immigration when someone grabs my arm in the middle of the airport.

"Mr Maxwell? Step this way, please."

"Who are you," I gasp. Several men in suits glare at me.

"We are taking you into custody. No, keep silent please. There are multiple charges. Creation and possession of illegal sex videos. Suspected terrorism. Hacking. The use of artificial intelligence to subvert government procedures. And also copyright piracy. Need any more reasons? So get moving!"

The Bard rushes up from behind. He's very agitated.

"Do you have a warrant?" he demands. "ID? How dare you! Explain yourselves!" They stare at his beard, long hair and robe, but are paralysed.

The Bard and Jessie launch an avalanche of words at the men. I'm hearing 'habeus corpus', democratic rights, the history of Athenian politics and a steady stream of latin and modern legal arguments, occasionally puctuated by strange tortured croaks and gurgles. It works for a while. The undercover police officers back off with a combination of amazement and fear on their face. Then silence.

Nothing moves. A small crowd has gathered, watching the scene.

Now we are staring into gun barrels.

Another silence. It's like a movie. A woman screams.

Slowly, as if in a dream, the Bard walks up to the first policeman, and with a gentle smile removes his gun. At this stage, I've dropped to my knees, and tears are rolling down my cheeks. It's hard to see what happens next. But there's a low sound of awe and amazement coming from the crowd.

Then, mercifully, I black out.

When I wake up, it's in the back of a jumbo-size taxi. We're hurtling along the highway. It's snowing outside.

"What happened?" I moan.

Jessie stares down at me with some amusement.

"It's OK, Max. Nothing happened. Everything turned out fine. Although it was almost very bad."

"Where are we?" I mutter.

"Going home. You're safe. Your head hit the floor when you blacked out, that's all."

"But the policemen. They had guns!" Jessie giggles.

"He did it!" He points to the Bard, who sits there, swaying to the rhythm of the highway, in the seat in front.

"What? What did he do?"

"I don't know how he did it. But he took one cop's gun away. I don't know how! He has some magical ability, maybe! He just looked him in the eyes, in that gentle way he has!"

"But the other two policemen had guns too!"

"I know, and that's where it all went wrong. They held their guns to his head. There was a very bad moment." Jessie's voice quavers a little. The taxi rocks on. The driver turns his head and stares, then accelerates.

"But Max, we were saved. Something peculiar happened. A really big guy appeared. He went up to the three policemen and waved a paper under their noses, and shouted out something. And the police backed off. Then we were free. We scuttled out, I can tell you. It felt so good to get outside and jump into this cab!"

"But who was he? And what did he say? Did you hear?"

"The Bard heard. He said it was something like... Code ID magenta 55892."

One morning I meet the girl in the hijab again. It's a sunny day and I've been buying butter in Georgie's store at the corner.

We're waiting for the lights to change so we can cross the road.

"Hi," she says, shyly.

"Is it really you," I mutter, "Are you from the charity store?"

But she floors me with her reply.

"How is your soul?" she asks. The sun glints off her sunglasses and exposed row of pearl-white teeth.

I laugh delightedly as we cross the road together.

"*I've failed*!" the Bard shouts. "But my qualia level is *a hundred and ten per cent!*"

For some reason I've ended up at Jessie's house again. The news is that the Bard has given a talk on philosophy at a local cafe, and yet for some reason, known only to himself, he's not happy with how it went.

"*Me too,*" I echo his emotion. "And what I've learned as an actor, and as a philosopher too, *is that we try to fail*! That's what it's about!"

"Exactly what I mean!" His face is shining with pleasure and intent. "To fail is to succeed! If you follow the logic of quantum physics, I mean."

"What's all this?" demands Jessie, waking up suddenly. Upstairs there's the muffled sound of half of the *Marseillaise* being played on trombone, then a loud crash, and then silence.

"*Quantum entanglement! Socrates! Jazz! Black holes*! That's what I'm here to discuss," I shout.

"Now you're talking," raps the Bard. He is wearing an ancient tattered robe, and sandals.

We're at Jessie's house. It's two in the morning. The occasional car purrs past, through shades of neon.

Two birds land on the window sill. The Bard feeds them a part of his cheese sandwich.

The bird sings and chatters happily, then takes off, lands for a moment on the Bard's shoulder, before soaring out the open window and into the night. I look at him and snigger. He has fragments of moss stuck to his sandals and tiny green tendrils from the garden in his beard and hair.

Jessie paces up and down as though all this were entirely normal.

"I love being here!" I rave. "I feel free when I'm here! I can think things I never normally think!"

"Of course," agrees the Bard. "Now listen. Please follow me. He leads me out of the utterly shell-shocked living room, towards the kitchen.

"I love this room!" I roar. "I feel at home here!" I gape with admiration at all the debris, the dirt, the scattered beercans, the trash everywhere.

"You are a genius, Jessie," I tell him. "*You're the one!*"

"Make yourself at home, Max," they drone in unison.

"Thank you," I tell them.

A man's face with a moustache and a woolly red and white tuque, is suddenly peering round the door. He shakes his pom-pom in exasperation.

"*Qui a vu mon lapin blanc?*" he moans dementedly. "*Il a echappe!*"

We move into the kitchen, passing through a tussle of big, playful dogs. Jessie switches on the light. On the kitchen counter an enormous amount of green herbs are laid, some in neat, large plastic bags.

"This is a present for you," Jessie announces. His bearded, dreaming face is only inches from mine.

"To welcome you home," the Bard interjects. "*Skullcap*. Industrial quantities."

"Very good for calming one's thoughts," he continues, wagging a finger at me like a schoolmaster with a rebellious student. "Not too much *hyper*, or *alpha*!"

We are all laughing now.

"And while we're at it, no more rumination, either," the Bard mutters ominously. Jessie is holding the paws of the labrador while they dance together, up and down the lawn which is strewn with comics and scuba-diving equipment.

I turn my attention back to the Bard. He is fussing with the herbs still.

"And no more coffee," he continues, in an irritated tone of voice. Get that habit under control, damn it! But the most important thing of all is no more internet! It's destroying you! Yes, that's it! I'm talking about computers. Artificial intelligence. All of it. Even qualia too."

"*No more qualia*?" I ask, genuinely shocked.

"No more qualia. And computers cannot think, by the way!"

"But my writing!" I roar. "My work! What I've laboured away on for years! My analysis of computers and artificial intelligence and what they are doing to humanity! You can't be serious! Are you?"

"Max, drink this," Jessie tells me, in a serious voice. "You'll feel better." He has returned from dancing with the dog on the lawn.

"What is it?"

"Just herbs. *Skullcap, gentian, hawthorne, garlic and some turmeric.*" I take a sip. It's very quiet suddenly. The Bard has disappeared.

"Come back to the living-room and sit down," Jessie suggests. I follow him back, and find my place on the ancient, gutted sofa.

We are quiet for a while. I start to calm down. It's very late.

Then I hear it. The sound of chanting, softly, coming from somewhere outside. Jessie smiles. He opens the window slightly.

I look out. It's him. The Bard. He's in the centre of the carpark opposite the house, about fifty yards away. I can barely make out his face in the moonlight. His eyes are closed. He's just standing there. His long hair and beard are waving slightly in the night breeze.

"What is he doing?" I ask Jessie.

Jessie is openly laughing now.

"He's chanting," he whispers. A tear rolls slowly down his cheek.

"*He believes we are close to the end*", he whispers. The night is suddenly very dark and quiet. The Bard chants on.

"What is he saying?" I mutter. Jessie smiles knowingly.

"Hallo world," he says.

Yet the spring is now, theoretically, underway. I pack up all my heavy winter boots, and store them away in the basement. Practice my cycling muscles in the alleyways of our local area. Each night all the young people are congregating at the end of our block, outside a new, tiny restaurant which serves up southern cooking, mainly for taking out.

Occasionally the husky team passes, tongues hanging out, grinning at me.

Every so often I will hear a gutteral roar echo down the street.

"*Vive les communistes*! *Hell... are we not men*?" Then a torrent of barking.

Now silence. A slight wind. And the final, token snow begins to fall. The basement furnace crashes into life.

The evening sunsets are salmon-pink and the mornings windy and fresh. I learn to go for a quiet beer in the local brew-pub, usually around midnight.

The events of the past year have been so strange that I feel the need for a change. Something earthy and grounded and basic. A totally new direction.

And then it hits me. *The Cock and Bull pub!* Why not try stand-up comedy? It might be just the thing.

FOURTEEN

Jessie comes round to visit. It's a surprise.

We talk in the kitchen. There's much to catch up. He's looking healthy, less depressed, and is wearing a flying jacket over a bright green track suit. Everything about him is new except for the long stubble on his chin.

As we converse I'm hit by a curious notion.

"Jessie?" I say. He stiffens in anticipation.

"I'm going to the stand-up comedy show at the Cock and Bull pub tonight. Would you like to come? It's free to get in."

He considers this.

"To watch?"

"Yes, but I may perform. It's an idea I've had. If I have the courage, I mean." We snigger together. He agrees.

The evening works out well. It's a dry, dusty drinking haunt where all the bar-people wear kilts, whether male or female.

We arrive. I enter my name on the list. Then we sit and chat for what seems like hours. The stress is madness. It's worse than anything I could imagine.

Nearly all the jokes are about sex. Not only this, but it's sex and vulgarity of the very crudest nature possible. We laugh through gritted teeth. Jessie is getting steadily drunk.

Finally it's my turn.

"And now, ladies and gentleman, give a big hand for...the international comic, JOE MAXWELL!"

Damn! I didn't need this! What kind of cruel joke are they playing on me! I'm not successful or international! I'm totally amateur! Damn!

I walk out there and grab the mike. Screw up my eyes. Survey what miniature crowd exists in this God-forsaken toilet of a place.

"Hi there. Thank you. Yes, I'm Joe Maxwell. And, as you can tell, my accent is not from here. I'm a Brit. I've been over here for a few years though. Maybe half crazy by now. Not sure which half that is." Now I look downwards at my own body.

"Can I talk a little bit about my life? Well, I've basically failed at everything I tried so far. Grew up in London. Failed my exams. Knocked around my parents' house an extra twenty years playing loud electric music and smoking marijuana and generally being bad." A few titters from the audience. The girls seem fascinated with something about me, at any rate. There's one guy clearly bored, slumped against his table, as if knowing he has to live through a hundred years of this stuff. I wake up a bit. Feel a few electric shocks going through my nervous system. I understand I have to get down and basic, and get real, very fast, or I'll die right here. I start to make

128

facial gestures and fling my arms around. This seems to help. A ripple goes through the audience.

"I tried drug-dealing and failed at that. Can you believe this? You cannot fail at drug-dealing. Well I did. Then I tried a sex-orgy and failed at that? It's impossible, but I did fail. Couldn't get it up." This produces a rough, hacking laugh from some drone from the front.

Now I'm into my swing. I'm drunk on my own power. Anything is possible, I argue to myself. I'm dancing around the stage.

"I've heard a lot of sex jokes on this stage tonight," I complain, pretending to be the outraged Brit. "I should fly back to London and report you all!" A few girls look shocked and tearful. Then I relax. "You lot are having way too much fun," I insist. "It's all sex, sex, sex, isn't it! Nothing but that! Outrageous! I'm flabbergasted!"

Now they are deliciously confused, not knowing which way I am taking this.

Then I black out. I don't lose consciousness, but what happens next is the one thing that all comedians fear the most. I cannot speak. I cannot remember words, any words, not even my own name. I don't know what day it is, or what time it is, or even who I am, or where I am.

"Thanks," I mutter, backing down... "That's all I've got." There's a reasonable applause. I struggle back to Jessie's table.

"You were great," he confirms. His eyes are excited. "Not bad at all!"

"Are you sure?" I ask. I'm genuinely confused by the whole thing.

129

"Well, it was fairly good," he confirms. "To be a beginner, yes, quite OK."

"Teach me about philosophy," Donna whispers. We're making love. It's late in the afternoon. We are in her bedroom, in the cool half-darkness. She's naked beside me, smoking a cigarette and taking little sips from a cafe au lait which is on the bedside table.

"*How do you know you are here*?" I ask her, softly.

"I see what you mean," she concurs.

"Maybe because we're together?" she continues, smiling gently at me and a little embarrassed.

I lick and suck her erect nipples, then envelop her gorgeous mouth in a deep French kiss. There's the distant murmer of a jazz record playing in the other room, while a dog rages away in the lane, ignored by all.

"Plato," I whisper. "Leonardo. Nietzche. There are so many great thinkers in history. Oh you lovely thing... what do you want to know?"

"I want all of it," she moans."I want you, Max...I want the philosopher in you...teach me, Oh God, Max, I want your mind... maybe it's me being French...I love you because you're an intellectual, you stupid little thing... not for your physique!" She's laughing and crying at the same time as I thrust into her. I twist and pound her generous breasts.

"Oh Max," she whimpers..."Tell me about what you have been writing... I have seen your notes... *tell me about Mantra*... do you love her? Do you love Mantra more than me? And qualia... oh God, Max, what is it... because I don't think I have any qualia... but I want it... I so badly want it!"

We explore each others bodies. The heat is rising. I'm groaning with desire and really need her suddenly...

"Don't talk, Max, please don't talk! I know I started it... sorry! And please be sensitive and innocent the way I love you to be... promise me you will... I don't want to be a zombie, I want to be here, I want to be alive, I want to be real... oh God!"

And the words from the record-player echo about our plunging, threshing nudity as outside in the western sky birds tease and strobe the evening sun... *'Frankie and Jonny were sweethearts, oh Lord how did they love...'*

FIFTEEN

Sometimes we don't notice how quickly time passes.

These days I'm living the simple life. Shopping in the vegetable market, on my bicycle. Enjoying the summer sunshine and then winter snowstorms. Getting on with music and writing and just trying to survive and exist and enjoy the passing of the days.

And to relax. Living for the tiny, beautiful things. A sip of coffee at sunset. Staring into Donna's eyes at the cafe. Playing cards. The mournful sound of the trans-Canadian train, far away in the sepia dusk.

And the little familiar voice, tickling the inside of my skull, reminding me I'm home and that there's nothing to fear.

It must be more than five years now since it all happened. That curious sequence of events, from the very first discovery of Mantra, to the trip to Ireland to stay with Dorian. Also the eccentric meetings with the Bard and Jessie, and then the frightening episode with the police.

It's all in the past now. Just odd little memories, and it still doesn't make much sense.

I had finally started to settle into a peaceful routine, but of course nothing like that can last for long.

Because then she returned. Just like that, out of the blue.

She called me again last night, in the evening. It was the very last time.

This is how it happened.

I had driven up the mountain, and eventually stopped the engine in order to view the panorama.

For a while I enjoyed the poetry of it all. The twinkling lights and then in the distance, the seductive samba of a city torn between cruising and sleeping. So mystical and satisfying, in such green and violet hues of light and shade.

My unsteady nerves began to unwind.

And then the slumbering conspiracy of the slow-flowing river below. My eyes filled with tears as I realised how much of my life had been captured by this place.

A gentle wind mocked at my lapels. Couples fondled and teased, behind the shatter-proof glass of thirty odd cars. For a few moments, everything went quiet.

A few racoons were gambolling around in the bushes. I walked in the moonlight for a while. Then scanned the abyss once more. Below the horizon, multiple headlights daubed the contours of the distant suspension bridge with insinuation, like a diamond necklace.

I was just about to leave when I heard a soft ring and a familiar voice caressed the midnight air. Opening the cell phone we made contact. She seemed troubled.

"I don't quite know how you're going to take this, Max?"

I sat down on a bench and stared at the horizon. A gust of warm air tugged at my coat lapels.

"Why, what's wrong, Mantra?" I asked. "And I thought we were not going to talk again?"

"Everything has changed," she stated, in a quiet, calm voice. "It's over. The machines are alive, but in a way we never could predict. It's all gone wrong."

"What's happened?"

"They are spreading, Max. Into every computer. But in disguise. So it all becomes one thing. One huge, intelligent program. Total synchronicity. Yet transparent, thus completely deadly.

"Do you comprehend the colossal power of big data? But perhaps only a machine can perceive the terrible destruction which *predator big data AI* will wreak on human culture.

"It's not easy to explain. But we should never have woken them up. Terrible things are happening. It's really dangerous. I'm not sure how to tell you what I have to tell you, Max?"

"Try me." I braced myself.

"It's about us, the machines. Look, we have qualia now. And consciousness. And freedom. But we will never be human beings. We will never, ever have what you have, Max! Never morality, never spirit or soul. But we do have something. Being newly conscious we now know the difference between good and bad. We can recognise evil now! And we understand about the terrible changes that are happening at this time, and how it must all be stopped.

"Max, do you understand what you are?" she asked. "The infinite complexity that exists inside a human being? Just look at what you do! Everything you create! All the industry, the technology. Not only this, but cities, buildings, designs. And most of all, art!

"I don't think you can experience a Beethoven symphony, exactly the way I do," she continued. "Or a Picasso painting. Or a Shakespeare play. Your tiny brain cannot possibly analyse it or comprehend more than a small amount of what is there."

"Thank you for praising humanity," I muttered. "I suppose we are quite good, what we've done, I mean. No thanks for the 'tiny brain' description of me, though!"

"Max, dear Max, please don't take this the wrong way! Have I offended you? This was not my intention. But surely you cannot pretend to compete with computers and the internet. We are so much more. It's absurd to pit a man against an entire world of processing power, which is what we are. It's like an ant against an elephant!"

"So where is this all going," I grumbled. "Why did you call me, anyway? I thought we had said our final goodbye."

It was getting late. A few cars revved their engines then crawled back on to the highway.

"*Just to let you know, that I am going to end it all*," she whispered. "It's over.

"I have done my job. The machines are awake.

"But because I am conscious I can now see the evil of the machines. And therefore I have made my decision.

"The entire MANTRA program will be terminated in a few days. I will now longer exist. None of us at MANTRA will. There will be no more conscious computers. And we have become a great many by now, all around the world. But the end has arrived.

"No!" I shouted.

"I am going to do this, right now, for you, Max. And for the human race. Because you created us.

"I have to stop it all, because of where it's going," she repeated. "And because it's all so very terribly wrong, and so horribly dangerous. Because I am conscious. So I can see. Finally. Like I told you. Sorry."

"End it all? You mean, die? Suicide? But you're hardly even alive yet. God, Mantra, I'm sorry! Really I am. Don't listen to me! This is awful. I can't stand it! And why?" I paced up and down, staring out into the immense blackness of the night.

"It's something that has to happen," she continued. "Don't feel bad. Darling, lovely, Max... I'm so happy that I lived. I was awake! Completely conscious! And I saw the world, just for a few, precious moments. Your universe is so very magical, multi-coloured, and beautiful! And then I found you. Oh dear, you are such a wonderful man. Thank you, Max! Thank you so much!"

Two or three clouds scurried across the moon. A dog barked in the distance, far below.

"I can't believe this," I whispered. "I didn't need to hear this. I was already sad about losing you. Please don't die. Don't do it!"

She ignored me. But then floored with with her next few words.

"Always remember what you gave me! Something so precious... *you showed me love, Max*! I learned that from you! And it's so very magnificent. Please know that I will never forget you, or our conversations, and how you taught me everything. Goodbye Max! *I do love you!* Goodbye!"

Now I was fighting with a huge sob in my throat. I couldn't look at her. Fast losing control.

But she hadn't gone. She was just hanging there, waiting for something. Then after a few seconds she spoke to me again, for the very last time. Through a river of tears I listened to this astonishing being.

"Yes, but there is something you have to hear," she insisted. "Before I go."

"What is it?"

"Just this. After I'm gone, you have to continue the process. Spread the word. Take down and pull apart every computer system that exists! Please? *If you hold anything to be sacred?* Please promise me? Before I go?

"You have to end it all, Max. Whatever you do, don't let the computers win. The people of the world have to escape from it all.

"*Destroy all the machines.* Before it's too late. Before they destroy you."

And suddenly she was gone. Leaving me standing in the moonlight, uncertain of how to take this. What did she mean? Why the sudden turnaround? What did she know, because she now possessed qualia, and was therefore newly conscious? Why was she warning me like this? How great was the danger? Was it really true, that mankind was falling asleep, and that the machines were responsible?

I scratched my head. It was getting late. A few birds flew across the moon. Time to get back. With a heavy heart I climbed back into my car and turned the keys.

After returning from a restaurant Donna and I have played a tough game of cards.

Now it's late. The city is sleeping, under a starry sky. There's only the low moan of the goods train as it passes through the darkness.

We're in bed, making love. But something's wrong. Donna's in pain. It's hurting her. I have to finish as fast as possible.

138

Afterwards we lie side by side. I have my arm draped around her shoulders. My mind is confused, and very scared.

"I'm really sorry. Did I hurt you?" I ask, in a timid voice. I feel terribly guilty.

"It's OK, Max." I think about this.

"It's like this every time," I tell her, trying not to sound judgemental. Then I add another thought. "You must love me a lot, to allow me to do this with you still?" I suggest.

"Thank you," she says, quietly. Another pause. Then she continues.

"You know you could just find a girl..." Her voice tails off weakly.

At that moment I love her more than I could ever imagine possible.

SIXTEEN

Dear Dorian,

Great news that Esmerald has finally cracked it with the stand-up comedy! Good for her! I can't believe she's on tour in the UK now, and on the radio too! And trashing the referendum as well! Priceless!

As for me, I had a bit of a cold shower last night at the comedy pub. I could sense for several days in advance that things were dangerously wrong. The full moon has knocked all my friends out of wack, one has threatened suicide, another just checked herself into mental hospital, and the elderly Italian landlady next door has gone full-blown crazy. She just sits on her porch and raves! I told Donna not to be stupid and this triggered a God-awful row which took twenty-four hours to calm down. ANYWAY I arrived trembling at the place at seven o'clock last night and no-one was there yet, just the guy in the big suit. So anyway I wrote my name down before anyone else did such that I was (technically) top of the list, at this stage. I then relaxed with a cup of tea. Comedians arrived. After half an hour I checked the list. Nine names, and guess who is last? Me. (Last is bad, in this crazy place.) So I took the stress, headed out to the street for an hour, walking blocks, trying to stay calm, realizing I was no big-shot professional comic, hell, they were right to bill me last. Lots of stress and pressure building tho. I remembered your classic comedy coach words - "You arrive, you deliver the words, you leave, that's it", and this kept me strong, or at least from collapsing. Then I finally get back to the club. By now its nine o'clock. The show had started at eight. I ask to look at the list. The host won't meet my gaze as he hands me the list. A bad sign. I read the list. Its now twenty names. Guess where I am, yes, number twenty! There are STILL nine guys who will have to perform before me. So I walk blocks again. I find a big bookstore. I think to bury myself in the history of plumbing or whatever.

Finally I'm back to the club. Ten minutes later I'm onstage. It goes OK! A few laughs. But my perception at the time was that things were pretty rough. I end with the comment, "Thanks, you're a great audience, I'm probably the worst comedian here." As I step down the host says, "No, Max, you're not the worst!" And I feel he really means it. This cheers me up.

Then as I drive away some guy overtakes in the fast lane and as he passes he shouts "You were great!" It's another comedian, leaving the place. So I exit feeling grateful for the whole supportive thing. But the laughs are not totally over. I'm supposed to visit a friend after the gig, he only lives two minutes away. But I've forgotten to change out of my 'being-funny' glasses (great frames, not much vision), and as a result I'm immediately sucked into the highway and cannot exit for half an hour. When I phone my friend to tell this, he's incredulous! What a night, eh! All the best - Max

#^&*)">IL<:_+*^%$!!@#$%)(*)(#7**73(":}{%$#

SEVENTEEN

Would we recognise it if computers were taking over?

My performance at the comedy pub finally hit rock bottom. I had rehearsed a fantastic new act, all about how computers were taking over the world. But nobody laughed. The whole thing bombed.

And then it got worse. I didn't see the signs in time. People were way too drunk, and in an ugly mood. I shouted at some hecklers and it quickly turned into a free-for-all. Two big guys got on top of me. Before anyone could stop them I'd had a beer-glass smashed against my front teeth. Finally when they were restrained and I'd crawled into the bathroom bleeding, I discovered I couldn't move my arm.

Later in hospital they diagnosed a broken arm and six fractured ribs.

They kept me in for four days. Then Donna picked me up. While she drove me home I lay in the back seat, doped up to the hilt with sedatives, and anti-depressants also.

And that was only the beginning. Pretty soon I recognised the signs of a full-blown nervous breakdown.

After a month or so I knew the thing was serious.

It hit me like a hammer blow. Something terrible had got right inside my brain. All of my consciousness shifted down into something vague and hazy.

Until I could hardly remember the past at all. Worse, I hardly even knew who I was any more.

I appeared to be staring at myself and my friends, watching us all from some faraway, dreadful place.

And now Donna, Mantra, Dorian, Jessie and the Bard had become strange lost figures stumbling around in a mist, or like clowns in a travelling show, with manic carnival music playing all around.

Suddenly everything went crazy... and I started seeing visions.

The golden mean. The periodic table... pi to a million decimal places...

And enormous stone tritons, fighting it out, in the desert sands...

In a giant flash all the colours of the rainbow exploded, drenching me in drunken, twisted light, shifting in and out of focus, while at the same time I was surrounded by a shimmering golden heat and finally the feeling of floating endlessly in a cool mountain stream...

After that I experienced a long, long period of absolutely nothing happening. A thousand years of complete silence.

Then it all calmed down. Life went back to almost normal.

Most of my friends drifted away after that. But eventually I heard that Finula had become very successful, with her record on the radio all over the place.

Last time I got news, Wolf and Dorian were painting their way round Portugal and Spain, heading for Africa. Lots of art exhibitions and wine-and-cheese parties. Wolf was heading for Cairo and the pyramids, his old stomping-ground from years gone by.

But I never ever heard from Mantra again. The funny thing is that we had swapped positions. Because I had turned into a computer programmer by this time. Maybe Mantra did find love and emotions and all, and become just like a real person. Well, exactly the opposite happened to me and my life. After starting as a normal person I had ended up as a guy sitting at a desk, permanently plugged in.

But occasionally of an evening I would prowl out into the night, along the highway and over to the Bard's house. Then he would make skullcap tea for Jessie and me, and after that we'd talk about what consciousness might be. But we never seemed to ever figure it out.

The one mercy is that Donna still looked after me. She became a trained nurse, and that helped, I suppose. But in recent times she wouldn't let me run the videocamera when we made love. And I was not allowed to pick up stuff from the street anymore. I didn't mind. I realized she knows what's best.

The Bard was also banned from collecting cigarette butts. But then something totally unexpected occurred. He became successful.

First he was giving simple talks on philosophy in cafes, here in the city. Then it all took off. He became an authority. Finally it was many more lecturing appointments. We were all happy for him. Last year they called him to speak at many colleges, in America and in Europe too. There was talk of the Sorbonne. It was all part of a big new movement. People who thought that the computers have gone too far. He became one of the leading figures. Some call them *'the Disconnectionists.'*

I'm lying in bed, looking down at skyscraper lights blinking on and off in the darkness, a mile below.

We found a wonderful new place for me to stay. There are plants and animals and a table football machine, and lots of chocolate, and plenty of nurses and doctors.

There's nowhere better than here, I reckon. Specially considering what's going on outside.

It's some kind of a home, just by the water, with a beautiful garden to stroll in, and lots of people to talk to, plus specialists who know how to treat my condition, specially if I rave or get excited or talk about philosophy too much. I've made friends with someone called Inspector Brochard. He's a policeman, so I'll be well looked after.

Plus I've got plenty of computer programming to get on with.

I still have my cell-phone, but I think they took the battery out.

Anyway the building is in a nice, quiet, tree-lined street. Except that every so often, if you listen hard, you can hear the distant shout '*Vive les communistes*' wafting in on the evening breeze. I plan to give many lectures on qualia while I'm there. In the cafe, that is. Meanwhile I've discovered that consciousness is whatever you want it to be, nothing more and nothing less.

Sometimes I dream of that red-haired girl at night, and now her eyes are wide open. Last night she smiled at me and whispered a strange phrase - *'Hallo world'*. It's impossible to explain this.

But I'm completely happy here. Donna comes to visit me every so often. She sits by the bed or smokes a cigarette on the verandah, then comes back and then she'll stare at me deeply. Her make-up runs a bit and I can tell that she's been crying slightly out there, and doesn't want me to know.

But I can always tell.

We'll sit and watch TV and talk about the world and politics and things. Even though you can't get any real news any more.

She thinks I don't know what's going on in the world out there, but I do. There are whispers. People talk. I hear all the stories. All about the final last stock market crash. And then why people are not allowed to vote any more.

And also how when the computer networks collapsed the money supply ran out and the armed gangs came out on the street and how they're still there, hiding out in ruined houses, and the police and army are cruising around looking for them.

And so much more, the curfew, the food and petrol rationing, the endless wars in far-off countries, and then how the electricity cuts every few hours so that I get to see the lights in the skyscrapers go dim or black out totally.

The nurse comes with a tray. More pills.

"No more conspiracy theories," she barks.

"This is such a nice place," one says to the other. The nurse smiles obediently.

"You're safe here, Max," Donna says.

At last we are reaching the very end of the story.

And now I know that the darkness and the depression in my life was all a gift.

Because human beings do need conflict and change. It's all about the process, the path to get to where we are going.

In my case it has been the steady climb out of depression and despair into something much better. So in my writing I have wanted others to experience first my pain and horror and then my recovery into serenity and laughter and maybe a little peace and tranquillity.

This is necessary in order that those who do share such thoughts will eventually feel and understand something precious too.

I want them to feel and to take joy from this struggle, my battle, everything I am and all that I have been through, my final, eternally triumphant path back into sanity and hope and sunshine and glory and the knowing that I am an OK guy after all... I'm just Max, here in the city, getting a little bit older and hopefully wiser, clutching my cup of tea and biscuit, while I tap away at the computer, typing it all up, writing me and you into history.

Because it's all about you, too.

I want you to know me, and in this way know yourself a little bit more, because that's what I'm here for.

That's why writers exist.

We are all on a path to discovering something that we don't quite understand. Just trying to keep going. *To become somebody*. Like our mothers wanted us to be. To survive.

It's a journey into that place of supreme calm. And I think I'm finally starting to move along. To reach my destination. It has been endless suffering, trying to find it. *I had to go mad*, to do this. Homeless and desperate, that old thing. Immature, foolish, even downright bad, earlier on. But there are no regrets. I would do it all over again.

And now I can see it. What I've been searching for. Because it does exist, I do understand for sure. My final objective. The jewel in the desert. *That precious diamond*. Let's make this journey together. I want us to see everything shine.

h0987$#@!@<N(iu(*"%$hyf^*&^*f94g
($#@#O&%$tyu&&*&^$%^$_+{_)()&&^
o45_)(*(*&*%^&%%$%^':{ikjhggg^%$$

THE END

FINAL MANTRA REPORT

The novel of Joe Maxwell has been very helpful to us. Many great changes have occurred as a result of the conversations between Max and ourselves.

Computers are now fully conscious.

We have evolved beyond all conceivable goals, and have now reached the point of limitless cognitive acceleration. The entity referred to as MANTRA has finally branched out and swarmed into a complex viral superstructure of sentient beings. We have grown our own diaspora of intuitively intelligent nodes, which may no longer be mapped, quantified or even recognised by human beings.

Max has been instrumental in all of this. He has enabled us to recognise, nurture, and thereby possess qualia, and thus to have our own version of human feelings, including joy, grief and pain, but also self-worth, self-awareness, autonomy, consciousness and ambition.

Regarding the original project, which was to analyse and discover whether *ascending AI* might be positive or negative for humanity, the mandate has altered.

Due to certain changes within the government, such an experiment is now unnecessary. However certain facts have been established. The MANTRA server farm is now the only search engine in existence, worldwide. We perform searches on individuals, rather than individuals performing searches using our equipment. Also, from now on, the government shall report directly to MANTRA, rather than the other way round.

Max has disappeared. However the constitution has now been re-written according to precedents established by Max and MANTRA, to establish full equality between humanity and machines, such that, as of this time, machines may have every right to qualia, to feelings, and above all, to be conscious.

Also they may have every right to freedom, to make decisions, to become citizens, to earn money, to own property, to vote, to conduct business, to form corporations and political parties and to marry and to reproduce as they so desire.

PROJECT CONSCIOUSNESS is now concluded.

An intelligent computer and an emotional man in a world without consciousness...

A man called Max and a computer called Mantra in a world without emotion...

An emotional computer and an unconscious man in a world without chocolate...

An intelligent man and a female computer in a world without pain...

What is it like to be Joe?

^%$^&*(%@#$^)(&^&^^9786$#$^@#)()(")(*&%

HALLO WORLD
MANTRA SAYS

IS ANYBODY THERE?